Rebecca Winters, an American writer and mother of four, was excited about the new millennium because it meant another new beginning. Having said goodbye to the classroom where she taught French and Spanish, she is now free to spend more time with her family, to travel and to write the Harlequin Romance® novels she loves so dearly.

Rebecca loves to hear from readers. If you wish to e-mail her, please visit her Web site at: www.rebeccawinters-author.com

Books by Rebecca Winters

Don't miss any of our special offers. Write to us at the following address for information on our newest releases.

Harlequin Reader Service
U.S.: 3010 Walden Ave., P.O. Box 1325, Buffalo, NY 14269
Canadian: P.O. Box 609, Fort Erie, Ont. L2A 5X3

RUSH TO THE ALTAR
Rebecca Winters

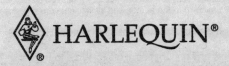

HARLEQUIN®

TORONTO • NEW YORK • LONDON
AMSTERDAM • PARIS • SYDNEY • HAMBURG
STOCKHOLM • ATHENS • TOKYO • MILAN • MADRID
PRAGUE • WARSAW • BUDAPEST • AUCKLAND

ISBN 0-373-03743-0

RUSH TO THE ALTAR

First North American Publication 2003.

This edition published by arrangement with Harlequin Books S.A.

® and TM are trademarks of the publisher. Trademarks indicated with ® are registered in the United States Patent and Trademark Office, the Canadian Trade Marks Office and in other countries.

Visit us at www.eHarlequin.com

Printed in U.S.A.

CHAPTER ONE

"HE WAS good-looking before in a dark, dashing way. Now he's handsome as sin, but you wouldn't want to tangle with a man fighting *his* demons! I'll do his vital signs before I leave the floor."

Riley Garrow had been lying propped in his hospital bed at St. Steven's counting the minutes until Bart Adams arrived.

Some of Riley's friends and colleagues as well as those of his deceased father had been in and out of his room at one time or other in the last two months. However faithful Bart, his dad's closest buddy and confidant, had been the one to serve as Riley's lifeline to the outside world during his convalescence.

But it was Sister Francesca's voice, not Bart's, he heard out in the hall. He had the strongest suspicion the head nurse had intended for him to overhear her.

Theirs had been an ongoing battle of the wills. Her psychiatric training hadn't prepared her for Riley's refusal to let her explore his inner self—the core, as she put it, where he really lived. The persona he showed to the world was a mere facade hiding the wounded soul struggling for help from within.

He loved baiting her when she started to pull her psychobabble on him. Since there wasn't anything else to do during the long boring hours, it made his day pushing her buttons.

"Uh-uh-uh," he would say to her, waving his index finger before her shrewd brown eyes. "Control, Sister.

Control. Don't forget you're a role model for the sweet young postulants under your care.''

At that point the gentle lines of her face would harden while she fought with herself to remain calm and collected.

"You're absolutely impossible,'' she would mutter before leaving the room in exasperation.

"I've been told that before by a number of women who've warmed my bed,'' he would call after her before bursting into laughter.

When she went off the day shift she briefed the night staff personally if they were new to the floor. After eight weeks and several plastic surgeries to graft skin from his leg to the area around his right eye and cheek, he knew everyone's schedule.

Unfortunately the only female nursing help who came and went from his room were lay nuns. That was something Sister Francesca had probably rigged up too. Surely there couldn't be that many women in Santa Monica, California, rushing to take vows of chastity and obedience.

He stared at the four sterile walls of his cage. "Sixty days without a real woman— No wonder I'm chomping at the bit to get out of here!''

"Your protest has been noted.'' Sister Francesca floated into his room pretending she was mother serenity herself this evening. "It appears heaven has heard your prayers at last, Mr. Garrow.''

He smiled up at her. "I didn't think heaven listened to *impossible* men.''

"They've made an exception in your case on behalf of all the sisters at St. Steven's who go to their knees the moment before they enter your room, and as soon as they leave.''

"All?" He arched one black brow. "Isn't it a sin to exaggerate, Sister?"

She started taking his vital signs. "After examining you on his rounds before dinner, Dr. Diazzo informed me you're being discharged in the morning."

Riley's eyelids closed tightly for a moment.

"I thought that news would please you."

He opened them again. "Since I know you'd be forced to do penance if you lied, I have to assume you're telling me the truth. For once I'm happy you invaded my privacy."

Her brows lifted. "For once I'm overcome by the admission."

"Don't let pride carry you away, Sister, otherwise you'll have to say extra novenas after vespers. Tell me—are you going to be here in the morning to make certain I never darken your doorstep again?"

"I'm afraid not. After the burden it has been taking care of you, I'm going on retreat with some other sisters."

"Where does a nun go exactly for a well-earned vacation?"

"That's none of your business."

"Ah, come on. You can tell me. I can keep a secret as well as a saint."

"If it will prevent you from bothering the other sisters, let's just say I'm returning to the Good Shepherd Convent for a short period of rejuvenation and study. I need it after the draining last eight weeks being in charge of your case."

Riley chuckled. "Rumor has it you're a devotee of Thomas Aquinas. He would be proud of you for following his example. You work in a hospital, serve the sick. You preach purity and peace to the heathen,'' he teased her. ''I'm partial to Francis of Assisi myself.''

''That doesn't surprise me. No doubt like him you've done your share of street brawling because of a misspent youth.''

''Would it surprise you to learn I even spent time in a Perugian prison?''

She took off the blood pressure cup. ''Nothing about you surprises me. Unfortunately the similarities between you and Francis of Assisi stop there, Mr. Garrow. His incarceration led to a spiritual conversion.''

''How do you know mine didn't? Uh-uh.'' He put up his finger. ''Don't judge this book by its cover.''

''It's the cover that has gotten you into so much trouble.''

If he weren't mistaken, her eyes took on a haunted look as she studied him. For a brief moment they reminded him of Mitra's eyes when she used to worry about him.

''I'm leaving the hospital, not dying, Sister. You won't be getting a last rite's confession out of me, but I do have a gift for you.''

''A nun doesn't ac—''

''Spare me the lecture,'' he broke in without remorse. ''This is one I guarantee you won't refuse.''

Acting as if she hadn't heard him, she placed a jug of fresh ice water from the cart on his bedside table, but he knew she was dying to hear more.

''You're not even going to ask what it is?''

''Need I remind you that for it to be a true gift, the right hand mustn't let the left hand know what it's doing?''

''I'm not the one striving for perfection. You, however, are very close to that sublime state and wouldn't dream of stooping to a petty weakness like curiosity. Therefore I'll tell you I've made a donation to your convent in honor of Sister Francesca.''

When his declaration penetrated, she bowed her head.

''You may not have succeeded in getting me to bare my soul, but you've convinced me there are angels on earth. Thank you for preventing me from giving up when I was at my lowest ebb. For that you've earned a permanent place in this sinner's heart.''

No doubt she was hiding her face because she didn't want him to see the moisture filling her eyes, another sign of weakness she was determined not to display.

As she turned to push the cart out of the room she said, ''Ever since you were brought in here, you've been in my prayers, Mr. Garrow. You always will be.''

''That's a comforting thought. With you as my advocate, maybe there's hope for me after all. Take care, Sister.''

''God bless you,'' she whispered before disappearing from the room.

No sooner had she left him alone than Bart entered.

''Sorry I'm late, but I think you'll forgive me when you see what I've brought you. I dug through my old things in the trailer to find this for you. It was published while you were working in Brazil with your father.'' He handed him a copy of *International Motorcycle World.*

The October issue from last year showed a female on the cover with a blond braid swinging below her helmet. She was riding through a farmer's muddy field on a motorcycle. There was a doctor's satchel strapped to the back. The caption read: *Even a modern day*

*American vet still rides an old Danelli-Strada 100
Sport Bike to work because they're built to last
forever.*

"Go ahead and take a look while I get us a couple
of soft drinks from the machine."

"Thanks, Bart."

The magazine had been printed the same month his
father had been killed doing what he loved best. With
an eagerness Riley hadn't felt about anything for a
long time, he opened the magazine. A small paragraph
on the inside about the cover said, "The children in
Prunedale, California, call her the 'mad' vet as she
rides around on her trusty cycle."

He chuckled before turning to the main article. His
first surprise came when he learned there were two
men involved in the creation of the original company;
Luca Danelli and Ernesto Strada. Riley had always
thought Strada meant it was a street bike because
strada was the word for street in Italian.

The story followed their fascinating lives from their
childhoods in Italy, through the World War II years
and beyond to the culmination of their dream to build
a motorcycle empire in Milan.

Riley and his father had always performed their
stunts on Danelli-Strada bikes. Then much to the motorcycle world's chagrin, all manufacturing suddenly
ended. His parent had insisted Danelli-Strada was the
only brand to be trusted and never could understand
why it had gone out of business.

"Listen to this—" Riley said as soon as Bart came
back in the room. "After Ernesto Strada died, Luca
Danelli lost heart, stopped production and dropped out
of the manufacturing scene." He put down the magazine. "So *that* was the reason."

The older man opened one of the colas and handed it to him. "Keep reading."

After swallowing the contents in one go, Riley picked up where he'd left off.

International Motorcycle World *has learned that once again Danelli motorcycles are being manufactured at their new headquarters in Turin, Italy. This announcement comes from CEO, Nicco Tescotti, who granted International Motorcycle World's chief staff writer Colin Grimes an exclusive interview.*

Racers around the globe are ecstatic in welcoming back this manufacturing giant after a long dearth. Already the new prototype called the Danelli NT-1 is clocking faster race times than any of the competition. Everyone else better move over because once again Luca Danelli is making his genius known. According to Tescotti, the company is here to stay.

Excitement swept through Riley's body. Maybe Sister Francesca's prayers for him hadn't been in vain after all. He lifted his head to find Bart smiling at him.

"I thought that article might put a light in your eyes."

"Might?" Riley blurted. "This has to be my lucky night."

"How come?"

"I was just told I'm getting out of here tomorrow."

"That's the best news I've heard since the plastic surgeon promised he could fix up your face like new."

Not exactly like new, but Riley could live with the subtle changes and wasn't about to complain.

"With this article I know exactly where I'm headed after I leave the hospital. You must have been inspired to bring it to me."

"For years now I've been aware you wanted to pursue your own career, but you couldn't do anything about it while your father needed you so badly.''

If Bart knew that, then he knew a lot more than Riley had given him credit for.

''I also happen to know the only reason you worked as a Hollywood stuntman for the last year was to make some fast, big bucks to pay off the bills he left owing.

''Now that you've accomplished your objective, I'm anxious to find out what you're going to do with the rest of your life. I figured the news about Luca Danelli would get your mind thinking. As I recall, Italy always did feel like home to you.''

Riley nodded. ''It *was* home to me for many years. Now I've got another reason to go back.'' There was one more debt to pay...

He eyed the other man for a long moment. ''Dad said you were the best friend a man ever had. He knew what he was talking about. Thanks for being here for me, Bart.''

The burly older man's eyes watered. ''I never had a wife or family. You kind of filled that spot, you know?'' he said in a strangely gruff voice.

''Until Mitra straightened me out, I thought you were my uncle.''

When they'd both had a good laugh, Riley levered himself from the bed to give him a bear hug. ''I promise to keep in touch with you.''

''That's all I needed to hear.''

''You didn't like *any* of the scripts I had sent over?'' D.L. thundered.

Annabelle Lassiter, known to her family and closest friends as Ann, met her agent's incredulous gaze across the lunch table at Pierre's without flinching. "I'm sorry, D.L., but I don't want to be typecast, and I don't happen to think any of these scripts are worth the paper they're printed on."

His thick red brows bumped together. "Listen to me—if you want to make a real name for yourself in this town, you'd better stop being so choosy. You may be a long-legged, classy looking blonde with a load of natural talent, but one successful film with Cory Sieverts doesn't guarantee a lifetime of work. You have to pay your dues, honey."

"I'm aware of that, but I refuse to act in a film aimed at sex-obsessed eighteen-year-old boys. That's all these are." She stared pointedly at the four scripts she'd put on the table.

"That's what's selling these days!"

"It's disgusting, D.L. I want something meaty like an *Anne of a Thousand Days*."

He pursed his lips. "A plum like that only comes along once in a decade. Even then those historical films don't always bring in the big bucks for the studios. You need to keep in mind you're already twenty-eight years old, that's over the hill for an actress."

"Thank you very much."

She knew it was true, but like any woman with red blood in her veins, she hated to hear it.

"I'm your agent. You pay me to tell you things like that for your own good. In your case you have to keep your name and gorgeous face before the public on a continual basis or it's curtains for you."

Maybe it was...

"Perhaps I should move to England and try to get work in the theater." It had been Colin Grime's idea.

Their long distance romance was difficult with him based in London and her in L.A.

D.L. looked scandalized. "You'd be a fool to do that when you already have a foot and a leg in the door here. Before you ruin what we've already got going for you, I have something else to tell you about. It's still in the works, but I can guarantee you a part."

"What is it?"

"A couple of writer friends of mine have been kicking around the idea of a survivor movie. It's strictly hush-hush at the moment. You'd be perfect for one of the older female roles.

"All I have to do is let them know you're interested. It'll be the biggest box office hit of the season. At that point you'll receive the kind of attention that will allow you to pick more of the type of projects you want."

"Thanks, but no thanks, D.L. That's not the kind of acting I've dreamed of doing since I was a teen. If you want to know the truth, I'd be ashamed to show my face in anything so crass."

His eyes squinted at her. "What happened to the woman who was one of those television contestants on, *Who Wants to Marry a Billionaire?* And what about that Hollywood benefit you were in, *Who Wants to Marry a Prince?* The one your twin sister had to make good on instead of you? You want to talk crass?" he bellowed.

Trust D.L. to hit her where it hurt most.

"I admit there was a time when I was so desperate to get noticed by a Hollywood mogul I'd do just about anything, but I've changed since then."

"You've changed all right." He got up and tossed three twenty dollar bills on the table. He was furious,

"When you're down to counting pennies again, don't phone *me*."

"D.L.?" she called to him before he'd stalked away with the rejected scripts. "I appreciate everything you've done to help build my career. Please don't be so angry that you write me off prematurely."

He eyed her for a long, uncomfortable moment. "I had you figured for someone a lot hungrier."

"You mean you thought I was capable of selling my soul." Pain shot through her. "It hurts to realize I gave you that impression. I have only myself to blame."

"You're damn right about that! When I get back to my office there'll be at minimum forty calls my secretary has taken since nine this morning from two-bit actresses who'd walk through fire to be in your position right now."

"I know." Once upon a time she'd been one of them. "Thank you for the delicious lunch. I'll pay next time."

"There may not be one."

"All I'm asking for is a decent script!"

"Don't hold your breath," he muttered before skirting the tables to make his exit.

As soon as he was gone, a dejected Ann left the restaurant and headed for her condo only a couple of miles away. After letting herself inside, she dashed to the kitchen to call her sister. But the red blinking light on the phone prompted her to listen to her messages first.

"Ann?"

It was Colin.

"How come you haven't been returning my calls? What's going on? I don't care if it's the middle of the night. Phone me, otherwise I'm getting on a plane to L.A. to find out what's wrong!''

He didn't bang down the receiver, but she sensed he'd wanted to. She couldn't deal with him right now and clicked to the next two messages from some actress friends of hers. After listening to their various plights, she punched in her sister's phone number.

There was a nine hour time difference between Hollywood, California, and Turin, Italy. It would be quarter to ten at night there. She doubted her sister was in bed yet...unless their baby Anna was being good and Nicco wanted some private time with his wife. He always wanted to be alone with her.

Ann had never seen a couple more in love.

Since her return from witnessing the christening of their adorable daughter a month ago, Ann had been experiencing a vague dissatisfaction with her own life.

The kinds of scripts D.L. had told her to look over only added to the strange emptiness building inside of her. She was almost frightened by the feeling because it reminded her of the way she'd felt after her father had died years ago.

She closed her eyes tightly. D.L. was right. She *had* changed in recent months. She'd been restless and out of sorts. Unable to focus.

In truth she longed for the comfort of precious Anna in her arms. The first time that tiny bundle of wiggling warmth cuddled up against her body, Ann's heart had melted. It had been a wrench to leave her niece when it came time to return to L.A.

Colin had attended the christening service with her. Afterward he'd accused her of caring more for the baby than she did for him.

''Ann?'' her sister cried out excitedly after picking

up on the fourth ring. "Nicco and I were just talking about you! We've been waiting to hear if you're contracted to do a new film yet."

Ann bit her lip. "Not yet…Callie? H-how would you like a babysitter for a couple of weeks so you and Nicco could go on a trip?" she stammered. "I know you could both use some time alone together. I promise to love her like my own and guard her with my life."

There was a pregnant pause.

"Until Anna's quite a bit older we couldn't bear to leave her for that long, but you don't have to be her babysitter to visit *us!*" Her sister sounded hurt. Callie always did have a heart of gold.

"As we told you before, there's a whole suite in the palace that will always be your home when you come. You can live here forever if you want. There's nothing I'd love more. You're the only family I've got, you know," she said in a quiet voice.

Ann did know. That's what was wrong. Callie was *her* only family and they were separated by an ocean. Tears stung her eyes. "Thank you," she whispered. "I don't intend to live with you, but I'm between scripts at the moment and—"

"And things aren't working out with you and Colin," her sister read between the lines.

Being identical twins made the two of them telepathic.

"Listen to me Annabelle Lassiter—you're getting on the next plane to Turin. Little Anna misses you terribly. We all do."

"As soon as I get off the phone I'll make reservations." She gripped the receiver tighter. "Are you sure Nicco won't mind? He must feel so stressed with all the responsibility now that Luca Danelli has passed away. The last thing he needs is another worry.''

''Don't be ridiculous. From the beginning he's been doing Luca's work along with his own. His death was very sad, but he was getting on, it was expected.

''Nicco's the one who told you you'd always have a permanent home with us. My husband never says something he doesn't mean.''

''That's because he's so in love with you, he wouldn't do anything to upset you if he could help it.''

''That's true,'' Nicco's rich male voice spoke into the phone, surprising Ann. ''But there's another reason and you know what it is. If it hadn't been for you, I'd have never met Callie.

''Because of you I've found my happiness. I love you, Ann. We both do. Let us know the number and time of your flight and we'll be there to pick you up.''

By now the tears were streaming down her cheeks. ''I love you both, too. Thank you, Nicco. See you soon.''

The sights and smells of any carnival grounds brought back so many vivid memories of Riley's childhood, he had difficulty believing he hadn't been swept back in time.

Before he'd left L.A., Riley had made a phone call to determine the exact location of Rimini's Traveling Circus. When he'd found out it was performing in Rome for the latter half of September, he'd booked his flight there.

That part was easy. The hard part was tracking down Mitra.

The circus Riley's father had performed in for close

to fifteen years was under new management. Though a few of the old troop members were still working, no one seemed to know what had happened to the Gypsy woman who'd once traveled with them and had read tea leaves for the crowds.

But Mitra had done a lot more than that. She'd been a surrogate mother to Riley though he hadn't recognized it at the time.

With a few more questions, Riley found out another Gypsy with a bear act had been added to the circus repertoire. He walked to the older man's trailer, speaking to him in the Romany tongue he'd picked up from Mitra. That broke the ice.

He learned she'd left the circus a year ago to join her own people in Perugia, north of Rome. The Gypsy had no idea if she was still alive.

After thanking him for the information, Riley left for the charming hill town overlooking the Tiber where he'd received his first formal schooling. It had all been thanks to Mitra who knew his father had been drinking heavily again after his third wife left him.

Though Mitra shied away from schooling, she'd said Riley was a *Gadja*, an outsider, and *Gadjas* belonged in the classroom.

Now he understood why she'd suggested that particular town. Years before her Gypsy heritage had brought her ancestors to the old Etruscan settlement that had become Perugia. The people who'd housed and fed Riley during those years his father struggled had been Mitra's extended family.

At first he'd fought his schooling and had gotten into serious trouble on several occasions. But with hindsight he realized she'd done him an enormous favor. He'd learned history and math, and of course how to speak fluent Italian.

None of that could have been accomplished without money which Riley's father didn't have. That meant someone else had to have put up the funds, probably at great personal sacrifice. Only one person would have cared enough about Riley to do that.

Once he'd revisited his old haunts, one of the men he remembered recognized him and gave him directions to her apartment. Thankful she was still alive, he hurried to her door and knocked. A deep voice called out in Romany, "Who's there?"

He answered back in kind. "Your *Gadja* child!"

In a moment Mitra opened the door. She was a medium sized woman in her late seventies now. She wore a familiar looking purple scarf around her hair which was turning white, but her black eyes were as alert as ever. They studied him with the same intensity that used to make him feel guilty if he'd done something wrong.

"You—" she whispered as if she'd seen a ghost.

He smiled. "You remember." He handed her a bouquet of lavender flowers he'd bought at a stall near the bottom of the hill.

She clutched them to her bosom. "Who could forget such a beautiful face? Now you are a beautiful man."

With her free hand she touched his cheek where the skin had been grafted. "I saw you in the tea leaves. I saw fire. Life has been hard for you."

"My father died last year."

She nodded, "I know. Come in."

Though modest, her place appeared comfortable.

She'd decorated the living room in the same vivid purple color he recalled seeing in her *tsara*.

"Sit down."

Riley complied while she put the flowers in a vase on her small dining table. Then she sank into the black hand-painted rocking chair he'd admired as a youngster. "How is it you have come to call on an old woman after all this time?"

"I meant to visit you long before now, but circumstances made it impossible."

"Life with your father has taken its toll on you."

"Let's not talk about me. You look well."

Her eyes narrowed. "You always were a good liar. You see the picture of us there? I felt good then."

Riley glanced at the framed photograph propped on the end table. The two of them had sat on a bench inside a doorless closet hooked up with a camera that took their picture at the carnival. He'd been six years old. She'd had black hair. A lump lodged in his throat to think she'd kept that photo all this time.

"I took care of you from the age of two until seventeen when your father left the circus and dragged you away. He should have left you with me."

With that statement he realized what a wrench that must have been for Mitra who'd never married or had children of her own.

"My father needed me too much and was jealous of my relationship with you. But even if he took me thousands of miles away, I always missed you. Did you get the postcards I sent you through the circus?"

She motioned to a black lacquered basket sitting on a bookshelf. He walked over to it and looked inside. It appeared she'd kept all of them.

Pleased to know she'd received them he said, "Why

didn't you get one of your family members to help you write back? I always left an address where you could reach me.''

''I didn't want to give your father any more reasons to make your life miserable.''

Mitra had understood everything.

''When he didn't drink, he was all right.''

''You deserved better,'' she muttered.

Riley took a deep breath before reaching in his pocket for an envelope. Enclosed was Italian lire amounting to five thousand dollars. Anything more and he knew she wouldn't accept it. He put it on the table next to the picture.

''What is that?''

He stared into her eyes. ''I know what you did. No amount of money in the world could compensate for the mother's love you gave to me. This represents a small token of my affection for you.''

Like Sister Francesca, she turned her head to hide her emotions. Whether disciplined saint or stoic Gypsy, both were women with hearts bigger than their bodies. Riley had been the lucky recipient.

''You once told me that if you could have your wish, you would buy fresh lavender flowers for your *tsara* every day. This apartment isn't the exciting Gypsy wagon I used to play in. It needs flowers. Now you can buy all you want.''

After an extended silence she fastened haunted eyes on him. ''You are in a great hurry, rushing down a path even more dangerous than the one before.''

He smiled and shook his head. ''Did you read death in the tea leaves for me, too?''

Her expression grew fierce. She made a fist and

pounded her breast. "Without a woman in your life, you're already dead here."

"There've been plenty of women."

A guttural sound came from her throat. "You think I don't know that? But they're always the wrong kind for my *Gadja!*"

"There was one exception," he drawled. "But it turns out she didn't want me."

"You mean she had too much respect for herself to fight a duel over you like those two she-cats? Good for her!"

"You have to admit that duel was really something." He grinned.

"Go ahead and laugh, but remember it was *I* who had to get you out of that filthy prison after the police carted the three of you off."

"I could always depend on you, Mitra. You know what the problem was? You were too old for me to marry," he teased her the way he'd done Sister Francesca.

She pushed her hand away as if to say, enough! "I have lived too long to find out you are still tormented. Go—"

Mitra always meant what she said. Nothing about her had changed except that she was twelve years older than the last time he'd seen her. He rose to his feet. "I'm leaving now, but I'll be back."

"Do not come again unless you bring me news I want to hear."

His expression sobered. "Unfortunately that's the one wish I can't promise to grant you."

CHAPTER TWO

SINCE Ann's last visit to Turin, a new sign in Italian spanned the two posts of the gate leading into the wooded property where Callie lived with her husband and worked.

Valentino Animal And Bird Preserve.

Lower down on one of the posts was another sign printed in Italian, English, French, German and Spanish.

This preserve is open and free to the public 7:00 a.m. to 7:00 p.m., Monday through Saturday. Stay on the indicated paths. Do not touch or feed the wildlife.

Please bring any homeless animals or birds who are sick or injured to the hospital by following the arrows. The hospital is open twenty-four hours.

After Ann had flown in from Los Angeles last evening, she'd gone straight to bed with a migraine. She always got one on a long plane ride. But this afternoon she was feeling much better and decided to take two-and-half-month-old Anna for a walk in her stroller before she got hungry for her next bottle.

To Ann's amusement, Chloe, her sister's pug, and Valentino, Nicco's boxer, decided to join her.

The four of them had started out along a private footpath at the rear of the small Baroque palace which eventually led through a security gate to the street. From there they circled partway round the property until she came to the public entrance to the preserve.

Following the arrows she headed for the eighteenth century hunting lodge located on the former royal estate. It had been converted to a hospital and stables. Callie did the main of her veterinarian work there.

When any animals or birds were dropped off with special nursing needs, she took them to the west wing of the palace. Nicco had remodeled several of the rooms into a kennel to board the sick or injured wildlife during their convalescence.

If the animal or bird could be saved, Callie brought them back to health. Then they were freed to live in the huge preserve with its giant trees, greenery and small fresh water lakes donated to the public by Nicco's younger brother Enzo, the ruling prince of the House of Tescotti.

Though Ann's agent had given her a hard time about her former willingness to do anything to get noticed by a talent scout, she wasn't sorry she'd entered for the *Who Wants to Marry a Prince?* benefit.

In begging Callie to take Ann's place at the last second because of an emergency, her sister had ended up married to the elder Tescotti prince who'd renounced his title so he could lead a normal life. Callie and Nicco were now a divinely happy working couple with a precious daughter and two pets they doted on.

Ann wanted that same kind of happiness. After being around them again last night, she realized she needed to end it with Colin. He had many wonderful qualities, but the fire simply wasn't there. To go on seeing him would be cruel. For both their sakes it was time to end it.

Only one man had ever made her feel she was about to go up in flames, and he'd been able to accomplish that by simply looking at her with those silvery eyes.

But he was the kind of man who set every woman's heart on fire. A rogue she'd instinctively known was not husband material.

She may have made a lot of mistakes in her life, but getting involved with Don Juan incarnate wasn't one of them, thank heaven!

While she stood there on the path wondering how to tell Colin the truth so it would hurt him the least, Valentino forged ahead. He knew exactly where to find his mistress. Chloe followed wherever Valentino went, prancing like a deer.

"Come on, Anna. We're going to have to hurry to catch up with them."

Halfway to the lodge she saw a dark head peer around the trunk of a massive chestnut tree. It was a boy of olive complexion and curly black hair who couldn't have been more than eleven or twelve. He was too thin for the worn-out white T-shirt and baggy pants he was wearing. His solemn black eyes swallowed up his piquant face.

Intrigued, she called out *"Buon Giorno!"* in her best Italian. Ever since her sister's marriage, she'd been studying the beautiful language on the side. If Callie was already speaking it fluently, so could she in time.

Her greeting must have frightened him because he disappeared behind the tree without saying anything. He was supposed to stay on the path. No doubt he'd come to the preserve without supervision. Taking it upon herself to investigate, she let go of the stroller.

Before she could reach him, he darted off in another direction, making it impossible for her to catch up to him. As she turned on her heel to get back to Anna, she saw a small black basket with a lid at the base of the tree. It wasn't like any workmanship she'd ever seen.

Curious, she picked it up and lifted the lid to see inside. As far as she could tell it was a baby squirrel, but it lay so still she had no idea if it was alive or not.

Had the boy come on his own to the preserve hoping for someone to help save it?

She looked all around for any sign of him. Except for the sound of birdsong and insects whirring about, nothing moved.

Tucking the basket under her arm, she walked over to the stroller and continued pushing it to the hospital.

Instead of entering the lodge through the main entrance to the waiting room, she went around to a private side door used by hospital personnel. It opened to an entry way leading into the surgery.

"There you are!" she spoke to the dogs as she opened the door for them to enter. The swinging door to the surgery had a window. She saw Callie over at the sink.

Ann tapped on the glass. When her sister spied her, she came out to the hall with a smile wreathing her face.

"All my favorite people!" She scratched the dogs' heads and gave her sleeping baby a kiss. Then she lifted her head to look at Ann. "What have you got under your arm?"

With a brief explanation about the boy, she handed her sister the basket. "Obviously he was too shy to come all the way to the hospital. I hope it's not too late for the squirrel."

"I'll check it right now."

"While you do that, I'll take everyone home and

start dinner. You did say there was chicken in the fridge.''

''Yes. Nicco loves it roasted with carrots and potatoes.''

''Mom's old recipe?''

Callie nodded.

''That'll be a cinch.''

''Put Anna in the swing so she can watch you. I should be home in time to feed her.''

''Okay. Let's go everybody.''

After leaving the lodge, she pushed the stroller back to the palace. The dogs raced on ahead, reminding her of horses who knew where the stable was and couldn't wait any longer for their oats and water.

Almost to the steps of the west wing, she thought she saw movement out of the corner of her eye. Something told her the boy had been following them, which meant he'd seen her drop off the basket at the hospital.

She felt a little tug at her heart. The squirrel couldn't be his pet because it was still a newborn. No doubt he had visions of raising it until it was full grown and would follow him around.

Through Callie, Ann had learned that people developed attachments to all kinds of undomesticated animals like iguanas and wombats. A squirrel didn't sound nearly so strange, especially if a boy's playground was the woods.

Growing up in farm country, Ann and Callie had been enamored of everything from baby chicks and calves to new foals. But if something went wrong with one of them, it was Callie who always wanted to doctor them.

Ann was a little squeamish in that department. One of her favorite pursuits was to spend time in her bedroom with their family dog. It was there she made up little plays she performed in front of him. He had to be a better audience than any human as he sat there watching and listening in adoration while his tail moved back and forth on the floor.

Good old Jasper. First he'd died, then their dad, then their mom. The home she and her sister had once known and cherished was gone.

With a heavy sigh she hurried inside with the dogs to take care of Anna and start dinner, very much aware that this was Callie's home, Callie's and Nicco's. Ann needed to make one of her own.

The problem was, you needed the right ingredients to come together at the right time and place.

So far that hadn't happened. Maybe it never would…

Getting closer to thirty every day with no man in her life she wanted to be the father of her children, plus a short-lived acting career in serious jeopardy, Ann realized she needed to do something about her situation.

If she were careful, she could live three more years on the money she'd made from her last picture. That would give her time to start looking for a job. Maybe she could teach. Might as well put her English degree and acting experience to some use.

Tomorrow morning she'd get up early and put out some feelers over the Internet in Callie's office.

On the outskirts of Turin, Riley found a compound of buildings that had to be the Danelli manufacturing plant. However until he saw the name in small letters on the glass door of the main structure, he would never have guessed he'd come to the right place.

Everything was locked up and the parking lot looked deserted. That didn't surprise him. It was ten after five in the evening. He'd tried to get here sooner, but after his flight from Rome there'd been a long delay picking up his rental car. The only thing to do was find a hotel for the night and return in the morning.

He walked back to the car and drove around the complex hoping to spot a worker or night watchman who could tell him when the best time would be to speak to the owner.

Luca Danelli wasn't listed in the telephone directory. All Riley could find was the name of the company and a phone number that reached a recording with only one option: leave a message and someone would return the call as soon as possible.

For what Riley had in mind, he needed the right live body. Nothing else would do.

Disappointed because no one was about, he whipped around the other end of the complex to leave the cluster of buildings the way he'd come in. That's when he caught a glint of red in the periphery and stood on his brakes.

A tall, well-honed male in a black helmet, gloves and leather jacket was just pushing a motorcycle out of a door marked private in Italian. Riley's eyes fastened on the fire-engine-red bike. It was an NT-1, the pro racing model that was blowing all the competition out of the water according to the article in the magazine Bart had given him.

Riley shut off the motor, grabbed the copy of *International Motorcycle World* lying on the seat next to him and levered himself from the car.

The man in the helmet had seen him. He raised his

shield. As Riley approached him, he was met by a pair of penetrating black eyes that studied him with guarded interest.

"The plant is closed. What can I do for you, *signore?*"

His Italian, as well as his whole demeanor, spoke of an aristocratic background, especially the way he'd phrased the question in civil tones to couch his demand. Riley was immediately intrigued.

Whoever this man was, he gave off an aura of someone so sure of himself, nothing fazed him. In an instant Riley realized he'd never met anyone like him. Instinct also told him something else. This was a person who welcomed a dangerous situation and would always come out the winner.

"My name is Riley Garrow," he answered in fluent Italian. "I've just flown in from the States to see Signore Danelli about a job. I came directly from the airport hoping he'd still be at work."

After a brief pause, "I'm afraid that's impossible now. The Danelli family buried him a week ago." The pathos in his voice revealed the two men had been close.

Riley's spirits sank like lead. "I had no idea. There was nothing about it in the news."

"The family has asked the press to hold the story until his only son who was injured in a serious small plane accident recovers enough to be told the truth."

"I'm sorry for them, and sorry for me," Riley murmured. "For years I've wanted to meet the man whose genius built the Danelli-Strada bike. My father taught me how to ride on a Danelli. Before he died, he refused to ride anything else and cursed the day the company went out of business."

He held up the magazine. "When I read Signore Danelli had started manufacturing bikes in Turin instead of Milan, I got on the next plane out of L.A."

The other man eyed him speculatively. "Who was your father?"

"You wouldn't know him. His name was Rocky Garrow."

"Rocky…" he muttered, "as in The Human Rocket?"

"You've heard of him?" Riley blinked in surprise.

"Of course. I thought your last name sounded familiar. As far as I'm concerned, he was the star of the Rimini Traveling Circus that came through Turin every spring. When I was a boy I couldn't wait to watch him do his motorcycle stunts over all those barrels. He looked exactly like a rocket in that shiny silver suit he wore!"

Riley smiled sadly. He'd given that suit and the other costumes to Bart who'd put them in storage for safekeeping. "When I got old enough to realize he wasn't immortal, I'm afraid I didn't want to watch." There were a lot of things he hadn't wanted to watch…

"I can understand that," he answered in a low, quiet voice. "I remember reading about his death doing a stunt over Iguasu Falls in Brazil last year. I'm sorry for your loss. He was part of the reason I fell in love with motorcycles in the first place."

Upon that admission Riley felt an intangible bond with the man.

He could scarcely believe this person had seen his father perform. He looked to be in his thirties, only a few years older than Riley. How strange to think of him as a boy in the audience while Riley waited anxiously behind the tent flap for his father to survive another jump.

"It was his time to go. He died on his old Danelli, doing the only thing that made him happy."

"Would that we could all bow out of this world the same way. It's a pleasure to meet the son of the man who gave me so many thrills in my youth. My name's Nicco Tescotti." He removed his glove so they could shake hands.

Nicco Tescotti?

"According to the magazine article, you're the CEO. I presume Signore Danelli's death puts you at the head of the company now. This is a singular honor for me, but not a good time for you with such heavy responsibilities. Forgive the intrusion."

As he turned to leave he heard, "Do you ride as well as your father did?"

Riley spun around. "Better!"

They both grinned.

"Have you had dinner yet?"

"What's that?" Riley fired back, too full of elation to consider his bodily needs for the moment.

"I prefer to discuss important business over a good meal. If you have no other plans for this evening, why not follow me home where we can relax and talk."

"I don't want to impose."

"You won't. My wife loves motorcycles as much as you and I do."

Riley smiled once more. Maybe he was dreaming. "She sounds remarkable, but she still might not want to be surprised."

"Half the time she surprises me."

"How so?"

"She's a vet. When I get home, more often than

not she's brought a baby something or other from the surgery we have to nurse through the night. And then of course there's our daughter Anna who's two and half months old. She's hungry for her breakfast at the crack of dawn which in turn wakes up the dogs.

"I'm afraid ours is not a conventional marriage." He got on his bike. "But I love it," he added with enough emotion for Riley to know Nicco Tescotti was one happy man.

"If we should get separated, ask anyone for directions to the Valentino Animal and Bird Preserve. The security guard at the gate will tell you where to go from there."

After closing his shield, he started up his bike. Riley chased after him in the rental car.

He recognized a pro racer when he saw one.

Though they might not be on the track, Nicco Tescotti rode with the kind of flawless precision and technique only a handful of the world's top racers demonstrated.

Riley tried to figure the odds of running into the new head of the Danelli company, let alone being invited to his home for a job interview. They had to be in the billion to one category.

"Keep saying those prayers, Sister," he whispered to the air as he stayed on the other man's tail.

Their journey followed the river back to the city. They'd been passing several miles of woods and verdant parkland when Nicco slowed down and signaled before making a right turn into a private driveway with a security guard at the gate.

Riley did the same. The guard nodded him on through.

Once past the thick hedge, he marveled at the ca-

thedral-like atmosphere of trees and shrubbery as the
path wound its way deeper and deeper into the greenery. But he didn't know real surprise until he glimpsed
a small Baroque palace beyond the dense foliage.

Nicco came to a stop at the entrance to the west
wing where several other cars were parked. He
climbed off his motorcycle.

Riley blinked. He lived here?

As he got out of the rental car, two dogs came racing out to greet their master. One was a fawn-colored
boxer with white feet who jumped up on Nicco's leg.
The other was a toy pug. It stayed at a distance and
barked with ferocity until Nicco removed his helmet
to reveal hair as black as Riley's. Then the pug leaped
toward him.

Laughter rumbled out of Riley. Nicco's chuckles
joined his as he scratched the ears of both dogs. Riley
moved closer.

"This big boy here is Valentino. Put your hand out
and he'll give you five."

Riley got down on his haunches and did as Nicco
suggested. The boxer was almost human the way he
hit his paw against Riley's hand. More laughter ensued
from both men.

The pug proceeded to run laps around Riley.

"Chloe, on the other hand, is a complicated lady
who hates my helmet and doesn't trust strangers. Give
her time and she might allow you to rub her head, but
don't hold your breath."

After she'd run out of steam, she sat there panting.
Riley had made pets of several stray dogs in his youth.
On impulse he put his hand on the ground and started
walking it slowly toward the pug with his fingers.

The dog made a strange cry in her throat, then got

down on her belly and shimmied toward his hand. Riley kept it going until the pug's flat nose came up against his fingers. She butted at him several times, then turned over on her back in invitation.

Triumphant, Riley began rubbing her belly. He noticed she was missing a toe from each front paw.

"The man with the velvet touch," Nicco murmured in awe. "Chloe's my wife's dog. She should be out here to witness this."

"I just did, and still can't believe it," a female voice answered in a tone of wonder.

Riley lifted his head, but he received the shock of his life when he found himself staring into the fabulous green eyes of the only woman in the world who'd ever turned him down flat for a date. Her rejection, delivered without the slightest hesitation, explanation or apology, had been a wound to his pride he'd never forgotten.

Annabelle Lassiter as he lived and breathed!

Less than a year ago she'd been the gorgeous American blonde on the set of the latest Cory Sieverts film, a big Hollywood box office hit. At the time there'd been no talk about her being married.

What in the hell was going on?

Nicco had said his wife was a veterinarian who loved motorcycles. They had a daughter Anna who was almost three months old. That meant she'd been pregnant when she'd cut Riley to the quick in front of the film crew.

The unpleasant experience still had the power to twist his gut if he allowed himself to think about it.

Had she become a vet before she'd ventured into acting?

How and where had she met Nicco Tescotti of all

people? A man with whom Riley already felt a rare camaraderie.

Why were they living on this palatial estate?

Reeling from a tumult of conflicting emotions, not to mention unanswered questions, he rose to his feet.

"Riley Garrow? I'd like to introduce you to my wi—"

"We've already met," he broke in before the other man could finish.

"We have?" Her expression looked totally puzzled as she clung to her husband.

A wave of anger swept through him.

She was pretending not to remember that incident at the studio, but he knew better. There'd been an attraction between them, a strong chemistry unlike anything he'd felt before. She'd felt it, too. It was something you couldn't hide, but she hadn't acted on her feelings.

If it hadn't been for the explosion on another set that had sent him to the hospital, he would have found a way to meet her again and break her down.

At the time he'd assumed she'd reacted as she'd done because the force of her feelings had frightened her. If they'd been anything like his, he could understand. She'd shaken his world, too.

If she was carrying Nicco's child, then it explained why she was so damn scared. Why in the hell hadn't she just come out and told him she was living with a man, or was secretly married?

This was a day full of shocks, both good and bad. Right now her acting ability was in full evidence. She even spoke passable Italian. No doubt she was praying he would let go of his determination to force a confrontation.

Out of deference to her husband, Riley decided to play along until the moment when he could get her alone to deliver a few home truths.

"If you don't recognize me, then I guess I'm mistaken. With that braid, you reminded me of someone I once met."

She hadn't been wearing her hair in a braid on the set. It had been arranged long and loose, like one of those cascading waterfalls in Brazil that caught the sunlight, robbing him of breath.

Nicco's eyes held a mysterious gleam. "Could you possibly be thinking of the woman on the cover of *International Motorcycle World?*"

At the question, something clicked in Riley's head. His gaze darted from the other man to Annabelle. "Of course—the mad vet from Prunedale!"

"That's my wife." Nicco kissed her neck.

"Up to my knees in mud." She blushed in her husband's arms. "I'm never going to live that picture down."

"It hooked *me,*" he said purposely in English because he wanted to jolt her.

Her eyes rounded, giving him the reaction he'd hoped for. "You're an American! I thought you were a hundred percent Italian like Nicco."

She spoke English now, playing the innocent to the hilt.

Nicco squeezed her. "Like you, my love, Riley's a man of many talents. He even has the distinction of winning over Chloe on a first encounter. I think I'm jealous."

"Dr. Wood won't believe it when I tell him."

"Dr. Wood?" Riley drawled.

She smiled. "He's the vet in Prunedale who hired

me out of medical school. He was the only person besides me Chloe would allow to touch her.''

''What about your husband?''

Nicco shook his head. ''Let's just say she was territorial about letting me sleep with my bride. It took her a week before she'd deign for me to stroke the back of her neck. I think it was a month before she rolled over so I could rub her belly.''

His black eyes flashed. ''If your secrets translate to the track, Riley, I'm already feeling sorry for the other poor devils when you start to make your moves.''

''So you race?'' she cried out with excitement.

She was good at dissembling. The best he'd ever seen.

''Never as a pro like your husband.''

''Why don't we finish this conversation inside?'' Nicco murmured against her cheek. ''I don't know about our guest, but I'm starving.''

''While you show Mr. Garrow where to freshen up, I'll check to make certain Anna's asleep, then meet you in the dining room.'' She slipped away from Nicco and hurried inside with the dogs at her heels.

No doubt she was relieved to escape before she gave anything away. He couldn't fault her for trying to make a go of her marriage.

Why out of all the many beautiful, exciting, exotic women he'd known in his life did he have to be hung up on the one female forbidden to him from the beginning?

Though he was no saint, he'd made it a rule never to become involved with a married woman. Little did Riley know another man had already claimed her when he'd met her on the set.

He supposed he should be admiring rather than angry of her devotion to her husband when Riley knew in his gut she'd once been as attracted to Riley as he'd been to her.

Riley was privy to a secret all right, one she didn't want Nicco to know about.

Back then the head of the Danelli empire hadn't won his bride's heart and soul yet, otherwise those green eyes wouldn't have come alive with desire for Riley when they'd first looked at each other.

He closed his eyes for a moment. He should have known this day was too good to be true.

You are in a great hurry, rushing down a path even more dangerous than the one before.

Riley liked Nicco. He sensed this was the kind of man he would want for a true friend. But under the circumstances, it wasn't going to work. The wisest course would be to heed Mitra's warning, excuse himself on some pretext and leave the country tonight.

"Shall we go in?" Nicco prompted him after parking his bike near the bushes. "Earlier in the day my wife told me Ann was making our dinner tonight. Between you and me she's not as good a cook as Callie, but she's a lot better than she used to be and she's trying hard to learn Italian. Be patient with her when she makes the effort."

Riley blinked. "Who's Callie?"

"My wife."

He was totally confused. "Then who's Ann?"

"My wife's twin sister. She flew in from the States last night for a visit."

CHAPTER THREE

ANN swept through the door connecting the kitchen to the small dining room of the palace carrying a hot platter.

"I'm glad you're home, Nicco. This chicken has been done for quite a while and—"

She suddenly stopped talking because she discovered her brother-in-law wasn't alone.

As far as Ann was concerned, her sister had married an Italian Adonis. There'd only been one man Ann had ever met whom she'd thought was better looking. To her shock that man was standing there in the flesh next to Nicco dressed in a stunning tan suit with shirt and tie.

The platter literally slipped from her hands to make a thud on the table. *"You—"* she blurted when she could finally say something.

His sensuous mouth curved into a cruel half smile of acknowledgment. Her heart might as well have been a gong going off in the background.

Gorgeous, hunky, devilishly dark and handsome with silver eyes... No matter how many adjectives came to mind, none of them adequately described Riley Garrow. Inside that powerful male body he possessed a virile essence. It could swallow you alive just by looking at him.

No woman was immune from his intangible charisma.

Lover today, gone tomorrow.

That was his reputation. It preceded him wherever he went as Hollywood's most sought after stuntman.

Oh, yes. She'd heard all about him long before he'd stepped foot on the set of her last movie. He was star material. Loaded.

No one could understand why he preferred to double for the hero in a dangerous scene rather than be the hero himself. No leading man had his matchless drawing power for women, his instincts for survival or his polish.

It was like some incredible dream to see him here inside the Tescotti palace of all places.

Worse, she felt irrational anger to discover he was even more attractive than she'd remembered. The line of his right eye tilted a trifle at the outer corner. When he stared at Ann through his heavily lashed lids, she felt seduced by his gaze and went hot all over.

What was it about men like Nicco and Riley who deliberately put their lives in mortal danger? How come they were better looking and more exciting than the average male? They might as well be a delectable poison.

Though she'd been tempted at the time, the rational part of her had been wise enough to turn him down for dinner after they were through shooting for the day. But her delight in thwarting him hadn't lasted long because he never came near her again. He never called. So much for a true interest in her on his part.

Once again she was thankful she'd spared herself the grief of spending an evening with him, only to find out he had plans with another woman the next night. And the night after that, ad infinitum.

No thank you.

She felt Nicco's speculative gaze. "It seems introductions aren't necessary."

"Not when it comes to the human cannon ball," she mocked, feeling flushed and totally out of control.

Riley shifted his weight as if welcoming her aggression. "You're referring to my father. He was the one billed 'The Human Rocket.'"

Still so smooth and unflappable, as if nothing could disturb him. Damn him for that cloak of sophistication he wore like an invisible mantel, setting him apart from ordinary men.

Nicco wasn't the only person to radiate a daunting indifference on occasion without being aware of it. Riley Garrow moved through life and women as if *he* were a prince of royal blood. The divine right of kings was alive and doing well inside him, title or not.

She wanted no part of him and sat down before either man could help her. "Shall we eat?" she suggested. "Anna was fussing, so it might be a while before Callie joins us."

Riley sat next to Nicco at one end of the table. She sat at the other end and began eating her salad while they helped themselves to the main course.

The stove in the kitchen heated differently than the one at her condo. Everything cooked faster here. She feared her roast chicken dinner was overdone. When Nicco passed her the food, one taste of the dry potatoes and she knew her meal was a fiasco.

To both men's credit they pretended to enjoy everything, but their guest overplayed his hand when he complimented her several times on the tasty chicken. To be patronized by Riley Garrow was the last straw.

At one point she happened to lift her head and met Nicco's puzzled glance.

"Perhaps you didn't hear about Riley's famous father. Around the same time Callie and I were married, he was killed doing a stunt at Iguasu Falls in Brazil."

Ann averted her eyes. She didn't know that.

"I'm sorry," she murmured. "Callie and I lost our father years ago, but it's still hard." There were still times when she missed him horribly.

Riley wiped the corner of his mouth with a napkin. "It's an inevitable fact of life we all learn to deal with one way or the other."

Growing more uncomfortable by the minute she said, "Are you planning to succeed him?"

Before he could answer, Callie entered the dining room and sat down at Nicco's other side. The dogs circled the table hoping someone would feed them.

"Forgive me for taking so long. Anna didn't want to settle down. She must know there's a guest in the house." Callie filled her plate. "This looks delicious, Ann."

"Thank you," she murmured, aware of Riley's unsettling gaze every time she happened to look up.

Nicco put a hand on his wife's arm. "I was about to tell your sister Riley has left his stunt work behind and is going to race for Danelli."

With her natural enthusiasm for the sport she loved, Callie said something about it being wonderful, but Ann's fork dropped on her plate. She stared pointedly at Riley.

"Out of the frying pan into the fire. Isn't that how the old saying goes? Except in your case I guess that doesn't apply since it appears you survived that, too. If you've had a death wish, it hasn't happened yet. Lucky you."

He didn't move, but his gray eyes turned molten as they held hers over the top of his wineglass.

"*Ann—*" her sister admonished in a loud enough whisper for everyone to hear.

Her head reared back. "Don't worry, Callie. Mr. Garrow knows what I mean. After he did the scenes for the film I was in, he was caught in an explosion on another set doubling as a firefighter and ended up in the hospital for smoke inhalation. All part of a day's work."

"That's horrible!" Callie cried. She shot Ann a withering glance before giving their guest her attention. "How long did they have to hold up the filming for you to recover?"

"As it turns out I was in the hospital two months, so they found a replacement to finish the picture."

Ann reacted too late to smother the moan that came out of her.

Nicco frowned. "Two months?"

"I received some burns that required plastic surgery to be done around my eye."

No one had told Ann how serious his injuries were, or that he'd been hospitalized for so long. She wanted to crawl in a hole for being so flippant about his injury.

Was that the reason he'd never phoned or sought her out?

When she realized what she was thinking, she was swamped by alternate feelings of shame for her behavior toward him, and fury at herself for still caring that he hadn't tried to pursue her.

"When were you released?" Nicco's concern was in full evidence.

"Four days ago. But don't worry. I worked out hard

in the hospital gym and the doctors have declared me fit to get back to any kind of work I choose.''

Callie shook her head. ''After your experience on the set, I don't blame you for choosing the race track. But I have to ask—didn't you ever consider normal acting?''

''I'm afraid I'd perish from such a life.''

Ann winced. He sounded as if he meant it. She didn't think she could sit here any longer.

''How amazing to realize you were in the same film with Ann. There were dozens of action scenes. Which ones were you in?''

Callie might be happily married, but she was fascinated by Riley all the same. As Ann had always known, no woman could resist him, not even her sister.

''He doubled for Corey in all of the hang gliding, underwater, horseback riding and motorcycle segments,'' Ann supplied grudgingly.

She knew she'd made a mistake the second Riley's eyes saluted her with a satisfied gleam.

Had he been able to tell she'd held her breath every time he'd done one of his death-defying scenes that took years off the lives of every cast and crew member who'd dared to watch?

''You were fabulous!'' Callie cried. ''Doesn't it unnerve you to see your own films when they come out?''

''I've never watched any footage,'' he declared flatly. ''The stunts I did were a means to an end, nothing more. My real interest has always been motorcycles.''

He and Nicco might as well be twins!

Stung by his frankness which proved he'd never

given her a thought once she'd turned him down, Ann pushed herself away from the table. "If you'll excuse me, I'll get the dessert."

"Those action scenes were incredibly impressive," Nicco continued talking as if she hadn't spoken. For him to be that complimentary revealed how excited he was for Riley to race for the Danelli team.

It meant he'd be living in Turin… Her heart thudded so hard she was terrified he could hear it.

"As Ms. Lassiter said, it's all in a day's work for me," she heard Riley explain once she'd headed for the kitchen with her plate. "But to answer your wife's question, the last time I went to a movie or watched a video was at least twelve years ago before I left Italy with my father."

"Where did you go after that?"

"Russia, Australia, South America. Anywhere there were carnival acts that would allow him to join them for a few seasons."

And he'd probably left a trail of broken hearts behind twenty thousand miles long.

Ann dashed over to the kitchen counter. With trembling hands she reached for the bowl of peppermint icing and began dropping blobs of it onto the chocolate cake she'd left out to cool. To her chagrin her motions were a little too violent. The icing broke through so the top of the cake resembled a bunch of potholes.

She smoothed it with the knife as best she could, but too much damage had been done. Crumbs had mixed in with the icing. It was a total mess.

Callie joined her a few minutes later with the rest of the dishes she'd cleared from the table. One look and she said, "I'll think we'll serve our guest gelato instead. Nicco can munch on his favorite cake later before we go to bed.''

''W-will you take care of it, please?'' Ann's voice shook. ''I want to check on the baby squirrel again. Maybe it will drink for me this time.''

''It's dying, Ann. You should have let me put it to sleep.''

''No!'' she cried emotionally. ''That boy brought it here hoping you could make it better.''

Ann rested the knife on the counter and hurried out the other door of the kitchen to the hallway which led to the palace rooms converted to a kennel. Once inside, she reached for a pair of rubber gloves and put them on before approaching the squirrel.

It lay in the kind of crib hospitals used for human newborns. There was a heating unit to keep the animal warm. Callie had hooked up an IV.

Everything possible was being done for it. Ann knew that, but it probably wasn't enough. Her sister had said the boy had brought it too late.

Still…

She was about to fill the eyedropper with some formula, but the second she saw the squirrel's position, she knew life had gone out of its body.

''Oh, no—''

A sob escaped her throat.

''I was afraid of this,'' Callie whispered behind her.

At the sound of her sister's voice, tears gushed down her face to wet her blouse.

Callie put an arm around her waist. ''What's going on, Ann? I'm not just talking about the squirrel.''

''Nothing.'' She pulled away from her to wipe her eyes.

''We were born ten minutes apart and spent eight

months together before that. When you hurt, so do I. Riley Garrow's the reason things haven't worked out with Colin. Isn't that true?''

''Why are you asking me all these questions?'' she cried in a strangled tone.

''I'll tell you why. After you'd finished making your movie, Nicco and I were expecting you to tell us you and Colin were going to be married. But it never happened. I knew something was wrong then. Now I know why. The poor guy doesn't know about Riley, does he.''

''No—'' Ann whispered, ''because there's nothing to tell.''

''Really.''

''Yes, really. We both worked on the same set, that's all.''

''No, that's not all.''

Callie would dig and dig until she'd pried everything out of her.

''He asked me out for dinner. I turned him down. That's it.''

''And you've been mad at yourself ever since because he didn't come back for more like all the others,'' she divined correctly like she always did. ''Now that I've met the one man in life who has managed to get past your defenses, I can see why Colin never stood a chance.

''Attractive as he is, he's no match for Riley Garrow. The only male on the planet who makes my heart race faster is—''

''Nicco—'' Ann blurted before her sister could. ''But there's one huge difference between the two of them.''

"You mean besides the fact that Riley wasn't born a prince?"

"No. In Hollywood the man has a reputation of being the original Don Juan."

"Well he would, wouldn't he, with his looks and the kind of excitement he engenders. As far as I know, it's not a crime."

"It should be," Ann grumbled.

"You have somewhat the same reputation you know."

Ann rounded on her sister. "What do you mean?"

"Your friend Alicia, the one who was at your condo the day I happened to phone, told me you've broken the hearts of quite a few guys including several hot new stars. One date and you're ready to move on to the next man. Of course I already knew that having watched you discard every date at home one by one."

Heat scorched her cheeks. "Don't compare me with Riley. I've never slept with any of them."

"I know that." Callie's mouth curved into a subtle smile. "I also know Mr. Garrow couldn't possibly have slept with *all* his legions of admirers, either. Otherwise he'd have been dead long ago."

"Even s—"

"Even so nothing!" Callie gainsaid her. "What else has you so upset?"

She sucked in her breath. "He's a human daredevil! Look what happened to him on that last film. And his father—he got killed doing one of his outrageous stunts over Iguasu Falls of all places!"

"But Riley's still very much alive," Callie persisted. "You heard him at the table. He's stopped performing stunt work."

Ann shook her head. "How can you say that when

he's going to start racing for Nicco's company? As far as I'm concerned, the racetrack is the original death trap.''

Her hands curled into fists. ''I wish there wasn't such a thing as a motorcycle. You're all lucky not to be dead yet—'' she cried in pain before leaving the kennel on a run.

Though moisture blinded her eyes, she managed to make it through the corridors of the palace to her bedroom on the second floor of the east wing. Once the doors closed behind her, she pulled off the rubber gloves and flung herself on the bed.

She sobbed angry tears, not only for her sister whose days were numbered if she continued to ride with Nicco, but for the boy who was going to be devastated when he found out no power on earth could bring back his baby squirrel.

Maybe in the morning she could talk to Callie about parting with one of the rabbits. Ann would put it in the basket with some food and place it under the tree.

The squirrel's sweet little face reminded her of a baby bunny's, especially through the eyes. Hopefully the boy would heal faster if he had another animal to look after.

Thinking about that brought her some solace. She finally sat up and smoothed the damp hair from her temples.

While she was at it, now would be the time to phone Colin and tell him she was coming to see him. He deserved to be given an explanation for their breakup in person.

She hadn't purposely dangled him. But now that her mind was made up, it was vital to put him out of his pain as soon as possible so he could meet someone else. Colin was a terrific person in his own right. They'd had wonderful times when they'd been together.

He'd begged her to go to bed with him. She'd told him she was waiting for marriage. He'd proposed several times. Living thousands of miles apart had made it easier for her to keep putting him off. He said he'd wait until she was ready.

But one chance meeting with Riley Garrow after all this time and she knew she'd never be ready. Not for Colin or any man.

Like Callie, Ann seemed to have a fatal attraction for one particular male. However in Ann's case he was a renegade who stole women's hearts when he wasn't embracing danger.

Riley's greatest thrill in life was to laugh death in the face. In between those rushes of adrenaline, any available female would do for a night's entertainment, then she was forgotten.

As long as Ann remembered he hadn't given her a thought since that day on the set, she'd be all right. There was no reason why she'd ever see him again anyway. She had no interest in Nicco's business which he conducted at his office or the track. Tonight had been an aberration from start to finish.

As it happened, she had her own business to take care of.

So saying, she reached for the phone and made a credit card call to Colin's flat in London.

Come on. Pick up.

To her chagrin she reached his voice mail after six rings and was told to leave a message.

"Colin? It's Ann. I'm sorry I haven't phoned befo—"

"Don't hang up!" He'd suddenly come on the line.

"Oh, Colin— I'm glad you're there."

"That makes two of us. Where are you?"

"I'm in Turin."

"Why didn't you tell me sooner?" He sounded hurt.

"This is the first opportunity I've had to get in touch with you since my arrival."

"Ann—we have to talk."

"I know. That's why I'm calling."

"I don't mean over the phone. Now that you've told me where you are, I'm flying there tomorrow. Expect me when you see me."

"No, Colin. I'll come to Lo—"

The line went dead.

She hung up the phone with the realization she should have flown to England first. It would be bad enough telling him goodbye at his flat, but so much worse doing it under Nicco's roof.

As soon as he arrived, she would urge him to take her for her drive. There were spots along the river where they could talk in private.

Knowing Colin, he'd probably come in the morning thinking they'd spend the whole day together. In that case she needed to be up early to see Callie about a rabbit for the little boy first.

She slid off the bed and headed for the bathroom to shower and wash her hair. If she had one thing to be grateful for, Colin hadn't shown up today at the same time as Riley Garrow.

Nicco liked Colin well enough and would have played the congenial host to both men at the dinner table. But Ann knew herself too well. She wouldn't have been able to handle sitting there in front of Nicco with a smile on her face for Colin while every molecule of her body was electrified by simply being in Riley's presence.

By the time she'd prepared for bed, she took a pill to ward off another headache she could feel coming on. To her surprise she slept well and awakened at seven in the morning filled with purpose.

She tied her hair back with a white scarf to keep it out of her face. After putting on a coral frost lipstick, she dressed in jeans and a gray pullover before hurrying downstairs and across the palace to the kennel.

Thankful Callie had buried the squirrel, Ann found the black basket sitting on the shelf beneath the empty crib and headed out the doors for the hospital.

The crisp fall air and clear blue sky made it a beautiful September morning. Too beautiful when she considered how Colin was going to feel when she broke her news to him. She wasn't looking forward to it, either.

"Hi, Dr. Donatti," she said as she walked into the surgery.

"Good morning, Ann. What brings you here so early on a Saturday?"

Dr. Donatti was the warm-hearted vet who'd worked for Nicco's family long before Callie had come on the scene. She noticed he was busy setting the left hind leg of a lovely marmalade cat.

"I guess you know about the baby squirrel."

"Callie told me. It's a shame the boy couldn't have brought it to her a little earlier."

"Do you think you'd be willing to part with one of the younger rabbits in the pen behind the lodge?"

"You mean to give to the boy?"

"Yes."

He smiled. "You're as soft as your sister. She already asked me the same thing last night before she went to bed. Go ahead and pick out the one you want."

"Thank you," Ann said with a lump in her throat. "I'm sure he'll take care of it, otherwise he wouldn't have brought the squirrel to the preserve for help."

"Let's hope you're right."

"I know you keep new portable animal cages in the storage room. If I paid you, could I take one to give him? I thought I'd fill it with some food the rabbit likes so the boy will know what to do."

"You don't need to pay for it."

"Well I'm going to!"

He chuckled. "Have it your own way. Look in that cabinet over there, third drawer down. There's a folder with some handouts in various languages for the care and feeding of rabbits. Find one to give to the boy, then take a sack and fill it with any other supplies you need.

"If there's one piece of advice to give him it's that rabbits like the cool shade and lots of water."

"That's what our dad taught us years ago," Ann said. "When they're too hot, you can feel the heat through their ears, so you have to wipe them with cool water."

"You should have gone to vet school, too."

"I'm beginning to think you're right. There's always need for a good one no matter your age. I'm afraid that's not true of a would-be actress who hasn't been a teenager for a long time."

He stared at her with a concerned expression. "Who told you you were too old?"

"My agent for one. It's just the way things are. I'm considering a career change."

"It's not too late to apply for medical school."

"I know, but I faint at the sight of blood. That's something that's never going to change."

She found the instruction sheet in question. After pulling out one in Italian and another in English, she rushed to the storage closet to gather timothy hay, alfalfa pellets and some fresh vegetables. When she'd assembled everything including a small cage, she hurried out the back door of the surgery to the pen.

There were over a dozen new rabbits, some white, some brown. She thought he'd prefer a brown one and let herself inside to catch one. It reminded her of times during her childhood when she and her friends chased farm animals around. She experienced a strong pang of nostalgia while she ran down one little guy.

In a few minutes she was successful, but the cute thing's nose quivered constantly from fear. She closed the pen door, then placed the rabbit carefully in the lacquered basket and put on the lid. Once that was done she hurried as fast as she could toward the entrance to the preserve juggling everything in her arms.

If the boy didn't come right away, she'd put the rabbit in the carrier and take everything back to the pen until tomorrow when she'd try it again.

She hadn't been walking long when she saw something dart through the woods to her right. It might be a deer, but it might also be… It was!

Excited, she kept moving until she came to the giant chestnut tree where she deposited her load at its base. Then she waited.

Pretty soon she saw the boy peeking at her from behind another tree. She beckoned to him. He seemed hesitant to approach. Using her best Italian, she told him to come closer.

When he still didn't move, she took the sheet printed in Italian and said the word rabbit to him, pointing at the basket. He called back a string of words she didn't understand.

"Rabbit!" she said again.

His face seemed to crumble.

"He wants to know where the squirrel is," a male voice sounded behind her.

Ann wheeled around to discover Riley Garrow mounted bareback on Spirito, Enzo's favorite gelding. Nicco's guest was dressed in jeans and a black T-shirt. He looked so incredibly handsome astride the magnificent chestnut, she felt like she was going to faint from the sheer force of his presence.

Nicco must have invited him to stay the night. Already the two men had forged a bond that shocked Ann. Her brother-in-law was always cordial to guests, but he was a private person and only allowed a few people into his inner circle. Somehow Riley had already managed the impossible.

"I've learned enough Italian to understand quite a bit, but I couldn't make out a single word the boy just said."

His eyes made a leisurely stroll over her features and hair, dissolving her bones. "That's because you're a *straneri*."

"What's that?"

"A non Gypsy."

"He's a Gypsy?" she whispered in surprise.

"That's right. He speaks Romany."

In the next breath he began talking to the boy in a tongue she'd never heard before. When in his life had

Riley Garrow learned to speak the language of the Gypsies?

While she was pondering that question, the boy wiped his eyes. Ann didn't need a translator to understand his actions. He was heartbroken.

"Tell him the bunny's face looks a little bit like the squirrel's and it will make a much better pet," she urged Riley.

His expression grew solemn. "The boy wants the squirrel. He saw the mother get shot and fall out of the tree with her baby."

Tears filled Ann's eyes. "The poor thing." She swallowed hard. "Explain to him I know how he feels. When our dog Jasper died, I wanted to die, too. But then our father gave us a little piglet to take care of that very day and pretty soon it didn't hurt so much."

Riley stared at her for a long moment. She couldn't imagine what he was thinking.

"Maybe if he could just see the bunny," she said on a burst of inspiration. Without waiting for him to say anything, she picked up the basket and took off the lid. Then she started walking toward the boy.

"Tell him this rabbit has never been away from its mother until now," she called over her shoulder. "If he'll take it home and care for it, the rabbit will love him and follow him around."

After a moment another conversation ensued. Again she marveled at Riley's language abilities. Still the boy stayed planted where he was.

Ann walked up to him, wounded by the pain in his soulful dark eyes. She stroked the back of the bunny which was huddled down in the box with its ears flat.

On impulse she reached for the boy's hand and

helped him stroke it for a minute. By this time Riley had sidled his horse up next to them.

She lifted her head to meet his eyes. This close she could see they were a crystalline gray, like clouds outlined in silvery flame. It was hard to breathe they were so beautiful.

"I want him to know this rabbit is healthy and won't die on him for many years. All it needs is love. That paper I brought will teach him how to give it the proper care. It's in Italian, so if you wouldn't mind translating."

Riley's gaze slowly left hers to rest on the boy. He spoke to him again. Their exchange went on for quite a while.

"He would like the rabbit, but he lives some distance from here and has no way to take everything with him."

"That means he slept in the preserve overnight. How far away is his home?"

"He lives in an encampment beyond the city."

"Would he let us drive him there? Then you could explain everything and we could meet his family. I could give them some money for more food and pellets. So they won't be offended, we could tell them it's a donation from the preserve. Part of their adopt-a-pet program."

One black brow quirked. "Is there such a thing?"

"Not yet, but if I know Callie that'll be the next project she discusses with Enzo."

He frowned. "Enzo?"

"Nicco's younger brother. Last year he became the ruling prince of the House of Tescotti. One of his first acts was to donate a portion of the Tescotti estate to the public for an animal and bird preserve. Callie's in charge.''

She moistened her lips nervously. ''That's Enzo's favorite mount you're riding,'' she added.

Her explanation seemed to have shocked him. ''I had no idea. That means Nicco is a prince, too.''

''He *was* once upon a time. But because he didn't want the life of a royal, he renounced his title in his mid-twenties and became a mechanical engineer. As you've found out, he'd rather design and ride *murder*-cycles than do the safe thing and run the affairs of the kingdom.''

His lips twitched. ''Something tells me you've never ridden on a...murdercycle.''

When he looked at her like that—sounded like that with his deep, velvety voice baiting her—she was in danger of forgetting who she was, or what she was doing.

Warmth stole up her neck into her cheeks. ''You're as astute as you are talented, Mr. Garrow. Will you please ask the boy if he'd like help getting all these things home? Callie will let me borrow her car.''

''There's no need to bother her. We can go in my rental.''

A sizzling tension was building between them. When she couldn't sustain his penetrating gaze any longer, she looked away. At that point he struck up another conversation with their young visitor.

''It's all decided,'' Riley said a minute later. ''He'll carry everything to the security gate while we go for the car. I told him we'd pick him up in ten minutes. That doesn't give us much time.''

Before she knew how it happened, Riley reached down and plucked her from the ground with the same matchless agility he'd displayed during the filming of his stunts. The next thing she knew, she was sitting in front of him on the horse.

His arm snaked around her waist and he pulled her tightly against him. "This is nice," he whispered against her neck as the horse headed back to the lodge.

Nice? There was nothing nice about it.

The touch of his lips sent shivers of ecstasy through her trembling body. By the time they'd gone the short distance to the stable, she was ready to jump out of her skin with the longing to be closer to him still.

CHAPTER FOUR

"THERE you are! We were just coming to find you so the four of us could ride together."

Ann opened her eyes in time to see Callie and Nicco mounted on their horses, ready for their usual morning jaunt. Dr. Donatti's wife Bianca was always up early to look in on the baby while they were gone.

Embarrassed to be caught with Riley like this, Ann jerked out of his strong arms and slid off the horse in one clumsy maneuver. The dogs rushed up to her.

Still quivering from the heated contact with him, she rubbed their heads to hide her shaken condition. When she got herself under some semblance of control she looked up at Callie.

"I—I imagine Dr. Donatti told you I gave the boy a rabbit and a cage. He needs help getting everything to his home. We're going to drive him because he lives too far away from here."

Callie blinked in surprise. Who could blame her after their conversation last night about Riley.

"We won't be long," Ann rushed to explain, transferring her gaze to Nicco. "I hope you won't mind my stealing Mr. Garrow for a little while. I'm afraid I don't speak very good Italian, let alone Romany. He speaks both with equal fluency and will be able to translate what's on the surgery printout for the boy's family."

Her brother-in-law's intelligent black gaze swerved to Riley's. "I'm glad word has reached the Gypsies

62

about the preserve. They're out in nature a great deal and probably come across injured wildlife more often than we know. It should have occurred to me long before now we need a sign at the gate in Romany. I'll give Enzo a call later.''

''We also need to print up instructions in their language,'' Callie said to her husband. ''Riley? How did you know the boy was a Gypsy?''

Ann watched him dismount with the kind of effortless male grace that was stunning to watch. ''The black basket. They're made by the Rom.''

He knew a lot more than he was telling. That was part of what made him such a fascinating, unforgettable man. Too unforgettable.

Don't get sucked in by him, Annabelle Lassiter. Just don't!

''We'd better hurry. The boy's waiting at the security gate.''

Riley nodded, drawing Ann's attention to his vibrant hair. It was as black as Nicco's, but he wore it a little shorter, probably because it had more curl.

''Give me a moment to walk the horse to his stall.''

''That's all right,'' Nicco murmured. ''I'll take care of him. You two go on.''

''Thank you. Please tell the Prince that Spirito lives up to his name in every way. It was sheer pleasure riding him.''

Nicco smiled. ''You're welcome to take him out anytime. These days my brother doesn't get to exercise him as much as he'd like.''

Ann trembled to think Riley might be a constant visitor to the preserve from now on. This couldn't be happening! She turned to the man who was responsible for the fluttery sensation in her chest.

"I'll run ahead for my purse and meet you at the car."

Without waiting for his response, she raced along the path leading to the palace. When she emerged into the dappled sunlight a few minutes later, she could hear his deep, rich laughter and discovered him doing tricks with the dogs who'd followed him from the stable.

At the sight of his powerful male physique, she slowed her steps to watch the play of rock-hard muscles beneath his T-shirt. A moan escaped her lips. She was as bad as any man who couldn't help staring at a beautiful woman. Worse even!

Chloe suddenly darted toward her bringing Riley's head around. Humiliated to be caught gawking at him, she bent down to give the dog's ears a scratch.

"Shall we go?" he prompted.

She rose up and finished walking toward him. He helped her in the passenger side and shut the door. Chloe barked when anyone left, but she finally gave it up to follow Valentino who had already run off to find his beloved Nicco.

Since Riley had followed her brother-in-law to the palace last evening, he appeared to know exactly where to go. After they'd pulled through the private gate to the street she turned to him. His handsome profile filled her gaze.

"Is this your first visit to Turin?"

"No, but it's been a long time since I was last here."

Ann had promised herself she wouldn't let thoughts of him take over. But it was a foolish promise she couldn't possibly keep. In truth she was way past the point of no return where he was concerned. Her interest in him had grown into a need she had to satisfy or go crazy in the process.

"Were you born in Italy?"

"Would you believe I'm a native Californian like you?"

Her breath caught in surprise. "What part?"

"Santa Monica."

So close to Hollywood. "When I was young I used to think how exciting it would be to grow up around the stars. Since then the blinders have come off. What was it like for you?"

"We didn't stay there long enough for me to find out"

"Why not?"

He fascinated her more than anyone she'd ever met, including Nicco, and that was saying a lot.

"When I was two, my mother walked out on my father and me."

The unexpected revelation was so painful to Ann she reeled in her seat.

"Dad never finished high school, but he and his friend Bart could do an impressive stunt riding routine on their motorcycles. They made enough money at various carnivals to stay alive.

"One of the owners of the Rimini Traveling Circus happened to be in the L.A. area looking over prospective talent. He caught their act and offered them a job in Italy. They took it and me, and never looked back.

"Dad once made the comment they were hired because they were riding Danelli bikes. Oddly enough it was the article in *International Motorcycle World* with your sister astride her Danelli on the cover that brought me to Turin. I was probably hired for the same reason."

The Danelli connection.

What she'd just heard explained Nicco's instant camaraderie with Riley Garrow. One man was born a prince. The other a pauper.

How hard his life must have been for him.

Her brother-in-law's innate compassion would have been deeply aroused by Riley's story, enough to offer him a slot on the racing team.

What Riley had shared with her had changed her image of him forever.

She cleared her throat. "When you grew older, did you ever meet your mother?" But she wasn't destined to hear his answer because they'd pulled up to the security gate.

"There's our boy," he murmured. Riley levered himself from the car to speak to the guard. In a minute he'd helped the young boy into the back seat with the cage and they were off.

Ann turned her head to smile at him. She was met with a stoic expression that hid his thoughts, yet his eyes didn't look quite as sad as before.

"Would you ask him how he knew to bring the squirrel to the preserve?"

After more conversation took place Riley said, "Every so often he fishes along the river running past the palatial estate across the highway. He's seen the hospital icon on the sign and watched people bring their animals."

He must have been living by his wits for a long time. "What's his name?"

When Riley asked the question, she heard their passenger say, "Boiko."

There was so much more she wanted to ask, but it was frustrating to have to use Riley to communicate.

He was a virtual renaissance man who could handle any situation no matter how difficult or unusual. So far she couldn't find any fault with him. Except one…

As Callie had told her, there was no law against being the most lethally attractive male in existence.

Ann's only defense against him was to avoid any more conversation until they'd accomplished their objective and she was back in her bedroom at the palace.

Before long they'd spanned the city limits. Riley knew exactly where to go as he took a road leading to an encampment of people. Ann estimated there must be several hundred tents.

The subject of her thoughts rapped out something in Romany. Riley pulled off the road and turned off the engine.

"You'd better stay in the car. I'll walk Boiko to his home."

"This was my idea. I'm coming with you."

His eyes captured hers. "You won't feel welcome here."

"That doesn't matter to me."

Without further discussion she opened her purse and pulled a hundred-dollar bill from her wallet. Then she got out of the car and opened the back door to reach for the sack of food. Riley took the cage while the boy followed with his new rabbit.

To her surprise he pointed to her and shook his head while he said something to Riley.

She thought she understood. "Why doesn't he want me to come?"

"You're a nice *Gadja,* but he's afraid his uncle will be mean to you."

Ann was touched by his words. She smiled at him, then turned to Riley and gave him the sack. "Please tell him that if he has any problem with the rabbit, to come to the hospital. If I'm not there, my twin sister will be. She's the doctor.''

After Riley translated, the boy nodded. While he stood there holding the basket with both hands, she rolled up the bill and stuck it under one of his thumbs.

''That's to buy more food for your pet when you've run out.'' She gave him a kiss on the cheek. Avoiding Riley's probing glance, she got back in the car to wait.

The two of them took off and were quickly absorbed into the crowd of people inhabiting the camp. Expecting Riley would be gone a while, she was shocked when he returned five minutes later carrying the cage and the sack of food. As he drew closer, she could see the rabbit was inside.

Something had gone terribly wrong. She felt a pit in her stomach.

Though she was anxious to know what had happened, she sensed Riley's reluctance to explain. Not wanting to frustrate him further, she remained silent for the drive back to the city.

About two miles from the preserve he expelled a heavy sigh. ''Those Gypsies are refugees who've made their way here from Slovakia. I don't believe the man Boiko referred to as his uncle is anything of the sort. Most likely he's a self-proclaimed leader of the group who rejected everything you gave Boiko out of hand.

''My instincts tell me the boy doesn't have any family left. As a precaution, I told him to hide the hundred dollars in his shoe. But God help him if he's caught with it.''

Ann swallowed hard. ''Why would the man care about a little rabbit?''

"Boiko has duties that don't cover taking care of another mouth to feed, even if it's a pet."

She winced. "What kind of duties?"

"Providing food any way he can. You did all you could, which is more than any other *straneri* has done for him. The boy won't forget your kindness. I wager he's already bragging to his friends that a *Gadja* who looks like an angel actually kissed him. He'll keep the money a secret."

Her head bowed. "He should be in school."

"There's the rub. The government has laws about children attending school who don't speak the official language. It takes money to educate them privately. Without language skills, they're not hired to work."

"How can they be if they've lost everything and have been forced to move thousands of miles from their homeland?" she cried.

"That's the other rub. The erroneous perception that all Gypsies are nomadic, owing their allegiance to no country, is still alive."

"Something needs to be done. They can't go on living under those conditions. They're unacceptable!"

"I couldn't agree more," Riley murmured.

Deep in thought, she didn't notice Nicco and Callie weren't alone until Riley had pulled to a stop in front of the west wing of the palace. The other rental car wasn't familiar, but the dark blond male visitor was...

"Colin—" she half-gasped his name. She'd forgotten all about the fact that he was coming to see her today!

He walked over to her side of the car and opened the door. "It's about time."

His voice sounded gruff before he pulled her from

the seat into his arms. In front of everyone he kissed her on the mouth.

Ann was so immersed in her own troubled thoughts, his kiss barely registered. When he finally relinquished her lips, his sunny blue eyes had darkened in shadow.

Over his shoulder her eyes met Riley's shuttered gaze. To her chagrin he moved around the car to join them. For an infinitesimal moment his features seemed to harden before he said, "Aren't you going to introduce us?"

"Yes. O-of course," she stammered. "Colin? This is Riley Garrow, the newest member of the Danelli racing team."

"So I understand."

Colin's withering comment was meant to intimidate Riley, but he had no idea of the kind of man he was up against. The situation was so precarious, she could scarcely function.

"Mr. Garrow? This is Colin Grimes. He's the writer responsible for the photograph and article you read in *International Motorcycle World*."

"I thought I'd heard the name before." Riley smiled, then extended his hand like the urbane host welcoming his long-awaited guest. It forced Colin to shake hands with him. "That was a sensational piece of work. It lured me from L.A."

"Any credit goes to Nicco who engineered the article with the same mastery he designs machines."

Ann felt Colin's accusing gaze as it swerved back to her. "I didn't know you two had done a film together."

She couldn't blame Callie or Nicco for this mess. Her family had been given no warning. Being with Riley since early morning had flustered Ann to the point that Colin had been the furthest thing from her mind.

"H-he worked with Cory," her voice faltered for a moment. "When he doubled for a scene, I stood and watched in horror like everyone else. If you'll excuse me for a minute, I need to put the rabbit back in the hutch behind the lodge. Then we can go for a drive."

The idea of the two of them spending another second in the same proximity as Riley Garrow was unthinkable.

"I'll take care of everything," Riley inserted in a smooth tone, reading her mind with uncanny ease. She watched him pull the sack and cage from the back of the car. He acted as if he lived here. It was no wonder Colin's body had gone taut with anger.

"Thank you," was all she could manage to say to him before he headed for the lodge.

Anxious to shield Colin from any more hurt, she put her arm through his. "Let's take a drive into the mountains. See you later," she murmured to Callie and Nicco who turned to go inside the palace. But not before her sister flashed her a private message of commiseration for the difficult task ahead.

Colin walked her around to his car and helped her in. Before long they'd left the estate. He merged with the traffic on the highway, then took the first exit that led them into the mountains.

They must have driven a half hour before he followed a sign to a small village. After finding a shady spot beneath a huge pine, he parked the car at the side of the road.

When he turned to her, his face was marred with lines. "Since the moment we left the palace grounds, I've been waiting for you to say something to me.

Anything! The fact that you don't have one word for me is more telling than you know.''

He'd stung her with the truth of his words.

''I was waiting for you to stop so we could look at each other while we talked.''

''And what do you see?'' he bit out.

''A wonderful man who deserves all the love of the right woman.''

He let out a strange sound. ''The classic rejection. I never thought I'd hear those words from you.''

''I think on some level you were waiting for them,'' she refuted him.

His head reared back in surprise.

''It's truth time, Colin, and the truth is, you met my sister first and fell for *her,* not me.''

''What in blazes are you talking about?'' he cried out, but she noticed he couldn't quite meet her eyes.

''You know exactly what I'm saying,'' she came back. ''That evening in Prunedale a year ago when Callie and I changed places so she could get away from Nicco, she gave me strict instructions. I'll tell you exactly what she said.

'''*You're going out to dinner with a very attractive man from* International Motorcycle World *named Colin Grimes. He's from London and used to race sport bikes. Now he's their head photographer.*

'*Nicco was in a rather foul mood when I left them at the Olivero farm, so pay more attention to him than Colin.*'

''I told her it sounded like her husband was jealous, and reminded her she ought to be thrilled with his response. It meant Nicco was insanely in love with her as she'd hoped. But Callie was too fearful at the time to believe it.

"The second I joined you and Nicco, I could tell by the way you responded to me that my sister's charms had already knocked you sideways. And trust me, Nicco noticed!

"That's why he was in such an impossible mood that night around you and me. He was still waiting for Callie to admit she was madly in love with him.

"Your interest in the wife he'd married so Enzo could be married and receive his title didn't help matters. Not when Nicco was already at his most vulnerable. He saw you as an attractive man who could be tough competition in case Callie didn't really love him back.

"Later on, after Nicco went after her and told her he couldn't live without her, you know what happened. She admitted her love for him and they returned to Italy to live. Everything's been perfect for them ever since.

"But not for you... I'm sorry you got stuck with the wrong twin."

"You weren't the wrong twin!" came his emotional declaration. "I wouldn't have asked *you* to marry me if I didn't love you."

"I believe that, but I also know you fell in love with my sister *before* you ever met me and discovered I'd been impersonating her. On a subconscious level I think you've been hoping I'd turn into Callie, the woman who lit your fire in the first place. But we know that's impossible."

Colin just kept staring at her because he knew what she'd just said was true.

"It's all right. At the time I didn't mind because I wasn't ready to get serious about anybody. Living so far apart made it easier for both of us to go on with a relationship that was never destined to end in marriage.''

''I'm sorry, Ann.'' He sounded devastated. ''I swear I never meant to hurt you.''

''You didn't. If I'd truly been in love with you, I would have stopped seeing you immediately rather than come in second best.''

After a silence he said, ''You changed during the filming of your movie. Now I find Hollywood's famous stunt man in residence under your brother-in-law's roof. The sparks flying between the two of you a little while ago speak for themselves.''

''He's not the marrying kind.''

''I have news for you. No man entertains marriage *until* the right woman tames him.''

And I have news for you, Colin Grimes. There's no woman in existence who could tame Riley Garrow.

''We should have had this talk last year, Colin. You're free to fall in love again. Who's to say what would have happened if Callie's heart hadn't already been taken by Nicco? Maybe you'd be my brother-in-law by now. But he got there first.''

''Tell me about it.''

''So, go back to London and find the woman who's been looking for you all her life. She'll be the luckiest woman in the world.''

''Ann...'' He grasped her hand and kissed the back of it. ''I want the same happiness for you.''

''I know you do. But not everybody is destined to end up married with children.''

He let go of her. ''You sound serious.''

''I am.''

''How soon are you going back to Hollywood?''

She lowered her head. ''I'm not sure.''

"For you of all people to be uncertain, you must be in love." He started the car and turned it around so they were headed for Turin.

"Let's not talk about Riley."

"I'm afraid I wasn't the one who mentioned his name. Now I have the answer to a question that has puzzled me for a long time. As long as I'm here, let's stop and have lunch somewhere for old times' sake."

"That sounds good. I'm starving."

Two hours later Colin drove her back to the palace. Because they no longer felt any pressure or guilt, their final lunch was the most enjoyable time she'd spent with him in months. He was going to be fine. That knowledge allowed her to walk away without regrets.

Before she actually made it inside the doors of the palace she noticed Nicco's motorcycle was gone. There was no sign of Riley's rental car either. That was good.

She was able to breathe a lot easier as she'd hurried through the palace to find her sister and tell her that she and Colin had said their final goodbyes.

After some searching she discovered Callie in the kitchen with Anna cooking up a storm. It seemed Nicco had just phoned and wanted her to bring dinner to the river later. Enzo and Maria were coming, too.

"That sounds like a romantic evening for the four of you. I'll tend Anna so you can stay on board all night. In fact you don't need to come back to the palace until Monday morning if you don't want to. Now that Colin's gone for good, I have no plans. Use me all you want for a sitter."

Callie shook her head. "When Nicco called from the office with the idea, he included you in the suggestion. I'd already told him you were probably going to break it off with Colin today. This is his way of trying to cheer you up. So, you can't disappoint him. Besides, he knows how much you love the barge.''

Love didn't quite cover it. If there was anything in this world Ann coveted, it was his barge. So far she hadn't found the temerity to ask if she could live on it when she came to Turin for visits.

Like everything featuring the Danelli name, the test track behind the plant was state-of-the-art engineering at its finest. Once Nicco had picked out a black NT-1 racing bike for Riley to try, he gave him a new helmet and racing gloves, then disappeared into his office, leaving Riley to his own devices.

Since Riley had the whole place to himself, he took his time testing it out. He wanted to get the feel of the changes Nicco had made to the original Danelli-Strada model that was setting the racing world on fire.

First he rode around to memorize the corners and straight stretches. The track temperature was perfect, not too hot, not too cold. At the same time he worked with the clutch and got used to the set of the foot pegs.

When he felt comfortable, he started doing laps. There was no chatter of the race spec tires, no problem with the throttle. The bike was a joy to ride.

Nicco's creation moved like a heat-seeking missile, smooth and sweet, seducing him almost as strongly as the feel of Ann's skin against his lips when he'd kissed the side of her neck.

His jaw hardened to realize she'd already been seducing Colin Grimes before Riley had come on the scene and been burned by the fire she'd lit. A fire that had refused to go out all these months and was growing hotter by the second.

Hell.

He began picking up speed to see what this monster could do. Soon he lost track of the time. His afternoon became a blur.

If he hadn't come close to running out of fuel, he could have done more laps. But all good things had to come to an end. When he leaned into the last curve and came around, he saw Nicco at the gate.

As Riley geared down to a stop, he glimpsed a satisfied smile shining from Nicco's black eyes.

Riley pulled off his helmet. "The bike is beyond perfection. It was like all the Christmases I ever dreamed of as a child coming true at once. I'm afraid I went into another mode out there."

"I'm glad you enjoyed the ride."

"Enjoyed doesn't begin to describe it. Ann told me you gave up the crown to design this baby. Perhaps the monarchy will never understand or appreciate what you've done for the motorcycle world, but if it means anything to you, I'm in awe of your genius, Nicco."

"I was going to say the same thing about your ride." Nicco eyed him intently. "I purposely didn't tell you this bike is fitted with a transponder. You clocked in doing a 1' 26' 66 lap time. That's faster than Vittore Loti's two test runs at Misano last month when he came in first both times.

"Up until now he's been our top racer. After today I have news for him. You're going to be our secret weapon at Imola on the twenty-ninth of the month."

Surprised and pleased to realize Nicco wanted him on the international racing circuit by the end of September, he levered himself from the bike and pushed it through the gate. The two of them entered the building where Riley parked it in a room with the other racing bikes.

He removed his riding gear and placed everything on the counter. Nicco operated the electronic device that locked the gate as well as the door of the building.

"On Monday we'll get you signed up and introduce you to the team members and crew who are in town. After you've been given a tour of the plant, you can pick out the street bike you want to ride to and from work."

Riley shook his head. "I won't take something from you I haven't earned."

"It's standard operating procedure," Nicco fired right back. "I want every member of the team riding one of our bikes when you're not on the track. It's the best advertising there is. Besides, you and I both know riding around in traffic keeps you sharp."

Nicco wouldn't lie to him about something like that, yet Riley still had the impression the other man had granted him some very special privileges.

"If that's the case, I'll keep my rental car till Monday morning."

"Good. When you return it, I'll meet you there in my car and drive you back to the office. In the meantime I would imagine you're anxious to see about a place to live."

"This weekend I planned to find myself some housing."

"I know of a spot that has Riley Garrow's name written all over it."

He sucked in his breath. "Enough, Nicco! You're probably the most generous man I've ever met, but there's a limit to what I can accept.

"You hired me before knowing what I could do on

the track. You took me to your home and have treated me…like a prince. I'm already in your debt much more than I want to be. I'll find my own apartment.''

"This isn't an apartment or anything close to it.''

"If you're talking the palace, that's out of the question.''

"As you're well aware, the palace isn't my first choice either,'' Nicco drawled. "However it makes the most sense for us to live there now that Callie runs the preserve. Before you say anything else, let me show you what I have in mind. If you don't like it, then you're on your own in that department.''

The man could move mountains and probably did on a regular basis. Riley would humor him until they reached their destination. At that point he'd thank him and turn him down. It wouldn't take him long to find an apartment.

However, like all things that had to do with Nicco Tescotti, everything was bigger than life and came as a total surprise, including a sister-in-law named Annabelle Lassiter.

Once again Riley found himself following Nicco into Turin. Before they reached the estate, he made a left turn toward the river and then took a private road that led down to a secluded marina.

To Riley's shock Nicco rode his motorcycle across a plank onto a small barge of all things tied up at the pier. The neat maneuver made Riley grin.

"Park your car and come aboard the Serpentine,'' he called out.

Intrigued, Riley did his bidding.

"Though I once kept an apartment not far from here, this barge was my home more often than not over the last ten years. It was my refuge from the world when it closed in on me. I remodeled it and worked on it whenever I found the time.

"When Callie came into my life, we honeymooned on this for three days, and spent a big part of our first year of marriage aboard her. It has every comfort of home with the added bonus of being totally private, yet it's able to navigate all the waterways.

"Unfortunately these days it just sits here because our lives have become more involved since Anna's birth. I'll never part with it, and intend to enjoy it in the future, but right now it's available.

"In truth, I haven't wanted anyone else to use it unless they could appreciate it the way I do," he added in a faraway voice.

There'd only been one place that had ever felt like a real home to Riley, where he'd known any happiness…it was the inside of Mitra's Gypsy wagon. That's because she'd been a constant in his life. Someone he could always run to for comfort and know she'd be there. Though she may never have said the word love, he'd felt it.

Oddly enough this barge Nicco had converted into a comfortable home on the water gave Riley that same kind of warm vibe. A prince who'd turned his back on his royal heritage to live a normal life had found a modicum of happiness here.

Lord, how Riley was tempted…

"Go ahead and look around while I set the table. Callie should be arriving soon."

"She's coming here?" He was still so bemused by Nicco's incredible offer he was slow on the uptake.

"Yes. I asked her to bring dinner. My brother and his wife will be joining us. I thought we'd take you on a short cruise. At night Turin is beautiful from the water."

CHAPTER FIVE

"WHAT'S Riley Garrow's rental car doing here?" she cried as Callie drove down the private road to the river bank.

"I have no idea." Her sister came to a stop behind Enzo's.

Ann's heart started to run away with her. "He didn't tell you he'd invited Riley?"

"No. Nicco said he had some work to do at the office. Later I saw Riley leave the palace with his suitcase in hand. I assumed he left to find a hotel. This is as big a surprise to me as it is to you."

Ann believed her.

"What's going on with your husband, Callie? I've never seen him treat his employees as if they were family," her voice shook. "I don't want to see Riley. I'll take Anna back to the palace with me."

"If you go home, it will hurt his feelings." She got out of the front seat and crawled in the back to lift Anna from her infant seat. "I don't think you realize how much he loves you. Because you're my only family, he'd move heaven and earth to make you happy."

"I know that."

"Then you need to know something else Nicco told me in bed last night."

"What was that?"

"He felt a strong connection to Riley the moment he learned his father was The Human Rocket."

"Why?"

"When Nicco was five or six, he had a favorite royal nanny who took him to the circus. According to him, it came through Turin every spring. He lived for it because Rocky Garrow was one of the stars who did fantastic stunts on his motorcycle."

"Good heavens," Ann whispered. The connection went as far back as that?

"Since Nicco always had to have someone guarding him, he learned to bribe whoever it was so he could stay to watch every performance. Riley's father was a superb cyclist who always used a Danelli-Strada to perform. That's where Nicco's love of motorcycles was born.

"On a subconscious level I think Nicco feels indebted to Riley's father. That's why he can't seem to do enough for the son."

With that explanation more pieces of the puzzle fell into place. But it didn't help Ann's state of mind. The man had gotten under her skin. Every time they were together, she found herself wanting to know more about him.

Thinking about Riley was almost as dangerous as being with him. She couldn't forget the feel of his arms around her or the thrill that ignited her body when he'd kissed her neck. No wonder every woman who met him thought she was in love...

Panicked by the thought of spending the evening around the man who was quickly becoming her addiction, she jumped out of the car and went around to the trunk to start unloading the dinner. Her only defense against his hold on her was to stay too busy to think.

"Something smells delicious."

Her breath caught.

Riley.

His powerful thigh brushed against hers. She imagined it was accidental and tried not to react to the contact, but it was so intimate her body trembled.

"The dinner actually *will* be, since Callie cooked everything."

Avoiding his eyes she handed him the large covered dripper. "Don't drop it or Nicco will go into mourning. He loves Sloppy Joes."

"So do I," came Riley's silky whisper. "I'll guard this with my life."

"What can we do to help?"

Enzo and Maria had arrived. With unsteady hands Ann indicated the cooler full of iced drinks. He lifted it out with ease and walked behind Riley to the barge.

Ann filled Maria's arms with the bags of buttered potato rolls, but the Princess didn't leave.

Speaking to Ann in excellent English she said, "Signore Garrow—he is very very good-looking. The most handsome man I have ever seen." Ann forced back a groan. "Please don't tell Enzo. It would hurt his feelings."

"Don't worry. My lips are sealed."

"What does sealed mean?"

"It means your secret is safe with me."

"Ah. When he wins his first championship, all the women will go crazy."

Tell me about it.

"I'm a little in love with him myself, Ann."

Confessions from yet another of Don Juan's would-be lovers. From the lips of a real live princess no less.

"He's so exciting," she went on enraptured. "I've told Enzo I want us to go to Imola to see his first race."

That brought a gasp from Ann. She felt as if a dagger had pierced her heart. Nicco had already put Riley on the team's schedule?

"When is the race?"

"Two weeks from today."

That meant he'd be leaving sooner to participate in the qualifying runs. The news should have brought Ann relief. Instead the knowledge that he was about to do something that could get him killed filled her with dread.

"Callie and Nicco are planning to go, too. You should join us if you're still here."

"I—I would if I didn't have other plans."

It wasn't a lie...not exactly. In two weeks she'd better have come up with another way to earn a living. Something that would keep her too busy and involved to think about all the horrendous ways Riley could die if another bike ran into him, or he crashed into the wall and burst into flames.

You didn't recover from an accident like that, not when you were charred beyond recognition.

"You go ahead, Maria. I'll bring the salads and the dessert."

Her hazel eyes looked at her with concern. "Are you all right? Nicco told me in private you have broken up with Signore Grimes. Is that true?"

Colin again.

Ann hadn't given him a thought since he'd dropped her off. It just proved how totally Riley had taken over her mind.

"Yes, but if I'm not quite myself, it's because I've decided to give up acting and get a job."

"Here in Turin?" She sounded delighted at the

prospect. Maria was a sweetheart. That's what Nicco always said about her. Ann agreed.

"I don't know yet. W-we'd better hurry and get on board or Nicco will come looking for us. Callie has her hands full appeasing his appetite."

Maria chuckled. "The Tescotti men love their food."

So did Riley.

A half hour later every bit of dinner had been consumed. While Ann had fed the baby her bottle, she'd noticed the Danelli team's brightest new star putting away Sloppy Joes with the best of them.

In between mouthfuls, Maria plied him with questions about his travels. The answers held everyone in rapt attention. Finally Nicco suggested they start their cruise before it got too late.

While Riley disappeared with Nicco into the engine room, Enzo undid the ropes. Callie and Maria busied themselves doing dishes. Ann volunteered to put the baby down in the bedroom. For once eight-month-old Prince Alberto had been left behind in the care of his grandparents.

Ann turned off the lamp and lay next to the baby. It felt good to stretch out on the king-size bed. Little Anna was so adorable, she didn't want her to go to sleep. But the movement of the barge as the current took them downstream worked like a sleeping pill. Anna's eyelids weren't the only ones fluttering.

The next time Ann became cognizant of her surroundings, there was no rocking motion, no sound of voices. The room was cloaked in semidarkness.

Still drowsy from sleep, she reached out to touch the baby, but her hand encountered a much larger body. One with muscles of steel. She cried out in alarm.

A light went on to reveal Riley half-lying on top of the bed looking at her through veiled eyes. Since dinner he'd changed into another T-shirt and sweats. He must have taken a shower on board. His black hair was still damp. Little tendrils curled at his temples. She could smell the soap he'd used.

Combined with the raw sexuality of the man, she felt overwhelmed. Even her breathing had grown shallow.

In a daze, she got to her knees. With shaky hands she smoothed the long blond hair out of her face so she could see the time on her watch.

"Seven o'clock?" Her gaze darted wildly to his. "Why didn't someone wake me up last night?"

"You were sleeping so soundly, I told Callie I'd drive you home later. As you can see, later never came. She said you needed the rest after your rough day with Colin."

Heat filled her cheeks. "I had no such thing!" Maybe she was dreaming.

"He really wasn't the right man for you."

"I know that!" she bit out before she realized how revealing her admission sounded. But it was too late to cover up now. "He fell in love with Callie before he ever met me."

"I heard about the great impersonation."

Good grief—did Nicco tell him everything? Apparently nothing was sacred!

"Colin liked both of us."

"The kiss he gave you was proof of that, yet I noticed you didn't put much into it. It's obvious you've moved on."

Riley didn't understand the situation. No thanks to Callie, he'd made it his business. That was too bad since the last thing she intended to do was satisfy his curiosity.

"You ought to know if anyone does," she said under her breath, but he heard her.

"You mean about moving on? You're right. I've done a lot of that in my time."

"I know. You were the topic of conversation on the set when it was rumored Don Juan was going to be doubling for Cory. In your honor someone coined the phrase, 'Lover today, gone tomorrow.' What's funny is, the women still keep coming back for more, don't they."

"Just like Colin. How many months did you string him along? A dozen maybe?"

"At least it lasted longer than your track record of…what is it? Twenty-four hours before you're off and running with a pathetic new hopeful?"

Ignoring her barb he said, "At least my conscience is clear knowing I don't work them over for a year at a time like you did with Colin. It'll probably take another twelve months out of his life just to undo the damage."

"Thank you for the compliment."

His white smile devastated her. "You're welcome. So who's the new man?"

"What are you talking about?"

"Your next victim. The one you wanted so desperately, you discarded poor, pathetic Colin whom you used shamelessly I might add."

Her body tautened. "Give me twenty-four hours. By then I'll have come up with a name," she mocked.

His hand whipped out to grasp her arm. With one

simple tug she fell on his chest. "You've got all of them down to the last second. I don't have to be anywhere else until Monday morning."

The wicked glint in his eye caused her heart to turn over. "No, Riley—I didn't mea—"

"Hush," he whispered against her lips. "Don't lie to me now and spoil it. We've both been waiting for this moment since that day on the set. Let's see how long it takes us to kiss each other out of our systems, shall we?"

His hands cupped her face, then his mouth covered hers. He made it impossible for her to escape his all-out invasion of her senses. Cocooned against his rock-hard frame, the pleasure was exquisite. Almost beyond bearing.

He rolled over on her to deepen their kiss. She moaned in ecstasy and clung to him, unable to stop what was happening.

Once Callie had told her that kissing Nicco was like being consumed by fire. He brought her rapture to die for.

Ann hadn't been able to relate to her sister's experience. In fact she feared she would never know the kind of mindless passion that swept you away, body and soul.

That was because she hadn't met Riley Garrow yet.

Tonight he made her feel as if she'd come alive for the first time. The last twenty-eight years had been nothing more than a prelude.

His mouth was doing incredible things to her. "Riley—" she gasped feverishly.

"I know." He groaned. "I feel the same way you do," he read her mind. "Twenty-four hours isn't going to do it for either of us. The only solution is to get married.''

Her green eyes flew open in shock. *"Married—"*

"It's a foreign concept to me, too.''

The comment tore her to shreds. She took a shuddering breath. "I don't want to marry you.''

His silvery gaze seemed to probe the deepest recesses of her being, sending a voluptuous shiver through her body.

"I don't want to marry you, either, but it's the only way I'll go to bed with a woman like you. Since it's what we're both dying for, we have no other choice.''

Her face went a scorched red. She tried to wiggle out from under him, to no avail. "I didn't fall asleep next to the baby as some sort of invitation!''

He made what sounded like a purr deep in his throat. "The invitation I'm talking about happened a long time ago, when we first looked into each other's eyes.

"Uh-uh-uh—" He silenced her mouth with another soul-destroying kiss. "Don't insult my intelligence by denying it. Once we're married the fire will burn itself out. It always does. Ask my father whose passion drove him to marry on three separate occasions. One by one they disappeared when the excitement was over.''

"Riley—" she cried in pain because his mother had abandoned him, but he kept on talking.

"At the point where you and I would rather do anything else than go to bed with each other, then we'll be able to look at our situation rationally. You can divorce me. I'll give you all my worldly goods and we'll part company with no bad feelings.''

"That's horrible!''

The beautiful, cynical man holding her in his arms terrified her. At the same time she wept for the child inside of him who must have gone through so much trauma growing up.

He gave an elegant shrug of his broad shoulders. "It's better than living in sin, so Sister Francesca tells me."

Ann stared up at him, heartsick over his admissions. "Who's Sister Francesca?"

His gray eyes softened like the early morning mist on the ocean. "She took care of me in the hospital. Afraid I was in danger of losing my immortal soul, she admonished me to settle down with the next woman who took my fancy. She said it was the only way for me to be redeemed.

"I thought about what she said." Riley's sensual mouth lifted at one corner. "Little did I know the heartless Ms. Annabelle Lassiter with her impressive collection of male scalps, would be the first woman I'd meet after leaving Sister Francesca's presence."

Suddenly lines marred his striking features. "You and I both know you took a lot more than my fancy that day. You owe me," he whispered savagely before kissing her long and hard.

He was insane.

Yet her desire for him drove away every instinct for self-preservation. It seemed *she* was the one insane with needs he'd brought to life.

"Think before you say yes or no," he whispered in her hair where he'd buried his face. "Depending on your answer, I'm out of here."

Out of here?

His threat filled her with consternation. She moaned in confusion and tried to get up, but he held her down.

"Riley—I don't understand—"

His eyes had darkened to pewter. "You're an intelligent woman. *You* figure it out."

If he meant what she thought he meant...

Aghast, her hands gripped his shoulders. "Y-you can't leave Italy now—not after Nicco's hired you to ride for the team!"

"Nothing's in writing yet."

She was starting to be afraid. "He invited you to his home! He's treated you like—like family!"

"And I've enjoyed every minute of it. Just remember he has a great head for business which is why he'll take it in his stride when I tell him personal reasons have forced me to look elsewhere for work. Being the remarkable man he is, he'll understand."

Ann shook her head in fear. "You wouldn't do that!"

He kissed both sides of her mouth, driving her crazy with desire. "In the last year I've been approached by two major companies. All I have to do is make a phone call."

Angry tears filled her eyes. "After everything Nicco has done for you, you would actually ride for the competition?"

"A man has to make his living somehow." His grimace convinced her he was serious.

Riley might be a fabulous cyclist, but after what Callie had confided in the car, there were hidden factors having to do with Riley's father that had prompted Nicco to go out of his way for him.

If Riley turned him down now to represent a rival company, it would be like throwing everything back in Nicco's face. She couldn't bear for her brother-in-law to be hurt like that.

Ann had watched the two of them interact at dinner. They were like old friends who were comfortable with each other and enjoyed the same things.

For two men who'd come from such different backgrounds and circumstances, they were so much alike, it was uncanny.

In her opinion one of the worst things in the world was to be disappointed in someone. Nicco had been so wonderful to her. In all honesty it made her ill to contemplate his being disillusioned about a man he genuinely admired.

How dare Riley put her in this position. "This is blackmail!"

"Call it whatever you wish," he said in an offhand manner.

Her hands balled into fists. "If I were foolish enough to marry you, where would we live?"

"Right here," he said in a smooth tone.

"On the barge?" Her voice came out more like a squeak.

"That's right. It's my home now."

She found the strength to push away from him and sit up. "Nicco *gave* you his favorite possession in the whole world?"

"Let's just say he made an offer I found too attractive to pass up. So I've arranged to rent it from him for an indefinite period."

For Nicco to trust Riley to this degree meant his feelings ran even deeper than Ann had realized.

New fears attacked her body.

"Don't you mean until you're killed in one of your death-defying maneuvers on the track?"

Deep laughter rumbled out of him. "If we haven't divorced by then, a fatal crash will save us the trouble.

In the meantime we're looking at as much loving as we can fit in. When I'm not at work, I'm all yours, sweetheart.''

''I'm not your sweetheart.''

She rolled away from him and stood up. The barge might be roped to the pier but she was so shaken, she felt like they were in a hurricane.

A tension-filled silence permeated the bedroom.

''Does that mean the answer is no?'' He lay there like a sleek black panther watching his prey through feral eyes before he pounced. Her heart leaped in her chest.

''Do you have to have it right this second?'' she cried.

''If you'd been the one lying helpless in a hospital bed for two months, you'd understand my impatience to get on with the business of living.''

Ever since he'd told them about his accident, Ann had been trying not to imagine what that awful period of pain and skin grafts must have been like for him.

In a lightning move he got to his feet and reached for his keys on the dresser. ''I'll take you back to the palace. Let's go.''

Her heart thudded with every step as she followed him out of the bedroom and through the cabin to the front of the barge.

He put the plank in place so she could reach the riverbank without getting wet. But when she would have started across, he picked her up in a fireman's lift and carried her to his car as if she were weightless.

After lowering her into the passenger seat, he kissed the nerve throbbing out of control at the base of her throat. Damn him for knowing where and how to touch her so all she wanted was him!

Once he'd climbed in behind the wheel and started the car, he didn't look at her again. When they reached street level she could see that the sun had come up over the horizon. Another beautiful fall day had dawned, but she was too full of apprehension to enjoy it.

Riley on the other hand appeared totally relaxed. He drove as if their vehicle was part of him, yet she sensed a certain determination about the set of his body that unnerved her. The closer they drew to the preserve without his saying anything, the more anxious she grew.

If she didn't agree to marry him, would he really renege on his plans to become part of the Danelli racing team?

Sooner than she would have liked, they'd pulled up to the west wing entrance of the palace. To her horror, he got out of the car at the same time she did.

She swung around in alarm. "Where are you going?"

"Inside. Last night your sister invited me for breakfast since there were no groceries on board. This will be the perfect time to tell Nicco about my decision to sign up with a different company."

So saying, he walked up the steps ahead of her and entered the palace as if he lived there.

Ann scrambled after him, terrified for what he was about to do. Those long swift strides of his had her running to keep him in her sights. Because he'd been here to dinner, he knew where to go.

If the fates weren't against her, Callie and Nicco might have decided to sleep in this morning. She prayed they weren't up yet.

He disappeared through the tall French doors to the

dining room. "Oh, good, Riley. You're here!" she heard her sister cry with real pleasure.

"You're just in time for my wife's hot apple fritters," Nicco chimed in. "While we eat, we can go over the stats from the latest race at Assen in the Netherlands. Where's Ann by the way?"

Ann burst into the room with so much momentum, the door swung against the stopper. The noise reverberated in every direction causing the dogs to moan.

Her family looked over at her in stunned surprise.

"I—I'm sorry," her voice faltered. "I didn't mean for that to happen."

Nicco grinned. "You must be hungry this morning. Come and sit down."

Riley didn't budge. "Callie? Forgive me, but I wonder if I could talk to your husband in private for a few minutes."

Silence fell over the room.

"Of course." She got up from the chair. "I'll go in the kitchen and make some more fritters. Come on, Ann. You can help me."

"No—"

Both Callie and Nicco eyed her as if they'd never seen her before. Riley's back was still toward her. If she didn't stop him right now, he was going to hurt the two people Ann cared about most in the world.

"Sorry," she said again. "Nothing's coming out right. Riley has this outdated notion that he should go to a male relative to ask for…my hand." Immediately Callie's expression changed to one of joy. "Since dad's not alive, he insists on talking to you, Nicco."

Her brother-in-law studied both of them for a long moment.

"You have every right to think what you're thinking,'' Riley said in a solemn tone, ''but I respect Ann too much to anticipate our vows. The truth is, I waited for Ann to wake up so I could drive her home. To my surprise she didn't come back to the land of the living until seven this morning. Since then we've been talking about our feelings.''

Ann's eyes closed tightly. They'd communicated all right. She felt like she'd been drugged by his touch.

''If it hadn't been for my accident, we would have gotten together much sooner.''

If only it were the truth, Riley.

''I did a lot of thinking in that hospital. Before I could do anything about Ann, I realized I needed to get on with my career plans first so I'd have something concrete to offer her.''

His lies were as outrageous as hers. They held her family spellbound.

''Finding her living beneath your roof came as a miraculous shock. I decided fate had placed her in my path a second time for a reason. We're planning to be married as soon as possible. It would be lovely to have your blessing.''

Nicco cocked his head. ''Since I kidnapped my bride and held her captive for a month while I courted her, I would be the last person to question your decision.''

He turned to Callie and reached for her hand which he kissed. ''What do you think your father would say, darling?''

''Dad didn't think any man was good enough for his girls. Of course he hadn't met you or Riley.''

She got out of the chair. After kissing her husband on the lips, she walked around the table. ''Welcome to the family, Riley. I couldn't be happier.'' She gave him a big hug.

"Amen to that.'' Nicco stood up and shook his hand. Ann could tell he was secretly pleased. "If you're in need of a priest, Father Luigi is available. He married my brother Enzo.''

"That would be perfect!'' Callie kept her arms around both men. "He and Maria will want to stand as witnesses. So will your parents. We'll need about a week to organize.''

Riley turned to Ann who'd been watching the three of them from a distance. He really was the most attractive man in existence. She would never get her fill of looking at him and he knew it!

Remember the marriage will only be temporary.

As Riley had said, when they reached a point where they'd rather do anything else than go to bed with each other, then it was all over. She wondered how long it would take before his desire for her waned. Probably not much more than twenty-four hours.

"I want what you want, sweetheart. Shall we set the date for next Saturday?''

Riley had said the one thing to convince Nicco he was dead serious about their forthcoming marriage. For someone who didn't love Ann and would make her a widow long before there was an opportunity to become a mother, Riley was carrying things too far.

His silver eyes pierced hers like lasers, daring her to say no.

Haunted by that unbelievable reality, she forced herself to nod. "Does that give you enough time to include someone you'd like to be there?''

She'd asked the question because her family was

listening. They expected her to behave like an excited bride-to-be in the planning stages.

"Yes."

Ann's heart started to hammer. She wanted to ask if it was his mother, but she didn't dare.

It really was going to happen. She was going to become his wife!

CHAPTER SIX

THE next week passed in a blur of preparations orchestrated by Callie who was crazy about Riley. Ann had no desire to buy any new clothes, but her sister insisted she do some shopping to augment her wardrobe. They found her wedding dress on Wednesday.

"I can tell you one thing, Annabelle Lassiter. You're not going to be married in jeans and an old top the way I was!" Her sister was emphatic about that. "This white chiffon is dreamy and looks like it was made for you."

Ann liked it well enough. The last thing she wanted was a traditional bridal gown with a train. Riley would find it mockable.

The normal length chiffon with the high neck and long sleeves would do fine. Handing the saleswoman her credit card, she said she'd take it.

"I think a garland of orange blossoms would be perfect for your hair."

"I'm glad you said that because I didn't plan to wear a veil."

Callie smiled. "I guess the shopping's done. Have you thought of something to give Riley for a wedding present?"

"N-not yet," she stammered. He'd probably laugh at anything she picked out. Ann would never forget what he'd said to her.

I don't want to marry you, either, but it's the only way I'd take a woman like you to bed.

She'd never forgive him for blackmailing her into submission...

"Well, as long as my mother-in-law is willing to keep Anna for the whole day, let's pick up lunch somewhere and eat it at Nicco's office. He'll have a good suggestion."

Ann hadn't spent five minutes with Riley since the morning he'd forced her into telling the family they were getting married. According to Nicco he was at the plant's test track during the day, then he rode his new street bike back to the barge alone after hours.

He'd purchased a cell phone and would call her in the evenings. Their conversations were abysmally short since Ann had little to say to him.

Callie had insisted Ann get a cell phone, too. Once they lived on the barge, it was the only way the two sisters would be able to stay in touch with each other.

Riley's excuse to Ann for not getting together with her boiled down to the fact that he was busy taking care of plans for their wedding dinner and couldn't trust himself to be alone with his intended bride.

She knew better.

He was having a weeklong bachelor party with some gorgeous woman he'd met. It would serve him right if Ann drove out to the river to surprise him, but she never managed to get up the nerve. The thought of discovering another female in residence, even if it was temporary, was too painful to contemplate.

It didn't take long to reach Nicco's office from the shopping arcade on the Via Roma. The thought of see-ing Riley caused Ann's heart to beat too fast the whole way there, but it almost flatlined when Nicco hap-pened to mention that Riley had gone out of town on personal business and wouldn't be back until Saturday.

After finishing his lunch, Nicco smiled at her from his swivel chair. "I'm sure he'd like anything you picked out for him. We have some sport watches here that are state of the art for a racing pro."

"I imagine she was thinking of something a little more romantic, darling."

His black gaze flicked from his wife's to Ann's. "Romantic..." He sat forward. "Let me think about it. I'll be home early."

True to his word, he walked into the palace kitchen at four where Callie had started to fix dinner. She was trying to talk Ann into the idea of eventually moving into the east wing of the palace with Riley. Their families could be completely separate, yet they'd be nearby.

Callie was being her wonderful, generous self, but she didn't understand that marriage to Riley wasn't going to be a normal one.

Besides, Riley wasn't the kind of man to live off of anyone else. After work on Monday, Nicco told them Riley paid him full price for the street bike he'd picked out to ride to and from work. He didn't want a free bike simply for being on the racing team.

Her brother-in-law would never have said anything about it if he didn't admire Riley for his principles.

He'd also shown his fierce independence in other ways by informing Ann they wouldn't be renting the barge very long. She didn't know what else he had in mind, but something told her the possibility of moving into the palace wasn't a consideration he would entertain.

After Nicco kissed his wife, he walked over to Ann and put his arm around her shoulders. "I've decided on the perfect gift you can give Riley. Come outside with me.''

"Wait for me!"

Callie followed them through the palace and out the west wing doors. Her steps slowed when she saw a new purple and lavender street bike. Nicco had parked it next to his red monster. It was the kind he'd designed with a lower seat height so the medium and shorter woman would be comfortable. There was a lavender helmet and gloves sitting on the seat.

She blinked. "I don't understand."

"Between Callie and me, we're going to teach you how to ride. Riley knows how much you hate motorcycles. It will blow him away if you learn the rudiments so the two of you can go on little trips together. That's one of the joys of life. I had one of the men at the plant drive it over."

Ann got this sinking feeling in the pit of her stomach. "No, Nicco—I couldn't!"

"I won't accept that," he fired back. She'd never heard him talk so sternly to her before. "Callie tells me someone you knew at your high school was killed on a motorcycle and it terrified you. I can understand that.

"But she also told me it was the sixteen-year-old's first time on a bike. He wasn't wearing any protection and had taken it out on the freeway without the tiniest clue of what he was doing. Those are the kinds of needless accidents that give motorcycles a bad name."

Ann had only seen Nicco *serious mode* one other time. It was the night he couldn't find Callie. He'd been a force you didn't want to contend with. This was the first time Ann had seen him this wrought up since his marriage. Whoa.

"Your husband-to-be is a true professional. He hasn't lived to the age of twenty-nine without knowing exactly what he's doing at all times. Rocky Garrow was probably the finest teacher a cyclist could ever have. Riley's his son and was born with his dad's instincts.

"The only accident that ever put Riley in the hospital was because of the explosion that rocked the set where he was doubling as a firefighter. You owe it to him and yourself to at least find out what it's like to ride one.

"I'm not even talking about riding on the street. There are hundreds, thousands of places off road in the mountains where you can have a lot of fun without the fear of collision or too much speed.

"You're an excellent driver, and Callie tells me you two rode everywhere on pedal bikes when you were young. There's no reason in the world why you can't ride a motorcycle with the same expertise once you've learned the fundamentals.

"My wife is a perfect example of someone who was taught the correct way. She practiced on the back country roads. In time, when she'd built her confidence, she was ready to be out on the freeway.

"If you try it and hate it, then so be it. But don't let one accident that happened to a kid years ago who didn't have the sense he was born with, keep you from an experience you might end up loving as much as your husband."

He's not going to be my husband very long, Nicco.

Even if she didn't lose him in an accident, she'd lose him when he decided he wanted someone else.

"Ann?" he prompted. "Have you heard anything I've been saying?"

"Yes, Nicco," she answered in a docile voice.

"If nothing else, you'll have a better understanding of your husband. That's vital if a marriage is going to work."

He doesn't love me. That's why it's not going to work.

She took a deep breath. Nicco had never asked anything of her, except for the time he'd forced her to show him where she thought Callie was hiding. That was a night she'd never forget.

After everything he'd done for her, what choice did she have now but to humor him?

Callie was staying exceptionally quiet. Ann didn't even have to look at her twin to know how much this would mean to her.

"How come you brought a purple one home?"

"Because I caught Riley admiring it the other day."

"Oh, all right!" she cried out in frustration. "But if I crash, I don't even own it."

He chuckled. "Let me worry about that."

"Okay...what do I have to do first?"

She'd never seen two people scramble so fast to enlighten her.

The helmet took some getting used to.

Learning how to work the clutch reminded her of those painful experiences at the farm when their mom taught them how to shift the truck gears. Ann liked the idea of her hands being in control of the brakes and the clutch.

Whatever Nicco had done, the bike seemed to be a perfect fit. After learning how to start the motor, she got used to pushing off. The hardest part seemed to be keeping her feet on the pegs. She had the urge to spread her legs in case she started to fall.

Pretty soon she was riding in big circles around the courtyard in plain view of them. She had to admit it was kind of fun, but she wasn't going to tell them that. Not yet. These were early days. Compared to the kind of riding Riley did at the track, she felt like a toddler trying to manage her first tricycle.

It was dark by the time she made her last circle around. Once she'd turned off the motor and set the kickstand, she pulled off her helmet and gloves to hand to Callie.

"I'm tired. Can I go in now?"

Nicco plucked her off the bike and swung her around in his arms. "That's my girl. I knew you could do it!"

My gosh! What was it about a motorcycle that sent men like him and Riley into ecstasy?

"Tomorrow we'll all ride around the track together after hours. I'll also take you on the back of mine so you'll be comfortable when you need to ride double with Riley."

What if she didn't want to?

But of course she wouldn't have dreamed of saying that to Nicco. He was acting as excited as a boy who'd just found his favorite toy under the Christmas tree.

Besides, she did wonder what it would feel like to go faster than a snail.

Later that night after her shower, she fell into bed exhausted. She'd been so tense learning how to ride, she noticed some sore muscles. While she rubbed them, the palace phone rang. Then a buzzer went off in her room. That meant the call was for her.

No doubt it was Riley. With pounding heart she picked up the receiver.

"Hello?"

"Ann—I've been looking all over for you. Why didn't you tell me you'd left for Italy?"

"D.L.? I'm sorry. It was a last minute decision."

"That's all right. I had your sister's number." He cleared his throat. "Listen, honey. I'm just on my way to lunch, but I have some news that will knock your socks off.

"They're going to do a sequel to Cory Sieverts' last movie. This is totally hush hush. I don't have official word yet, but it looks like you're going to be starring in another film with him as early as a couple of weeks."

She shot up in bed. That was the same time as Riley's first race at Misano. Since he had appeared on the scene, she'd forgotten all about her career. He'd managed to wipe her memory clean of everything but him.

"How come you're so quiet? This time we're going for the big bucks!"

She pushed the hair out of her face. "I don't know what to say, D.L."

"Hey—you're not on something are you?" He was starting to get upset.

Yes. I've developed an addiction for Riley Garrow. I'm afraid it's fatal.

"You caught me in a sound sleep. Of course that's great news," she said, but the thought of being in another film sounded awful. And she knew why. It would mean being away from Riley.

Dear God. She was in love with him.

"Ann?" he bellowed.

"I'm still here, D.L."

"How long are you planning to stay there?"

"I—I'm not sure yet."

"Well you'd better get home soon!"

"Will you let me know when it's official?"

There was a long pause. "Whatever happened to the woman who called my office every morning for any news at all?"

That woman no longer exists.

"Things are a little complicated here."

She didn't dare tell him she was being married. D.L. didn't know how to keep a secret like that.

The last thing she wanted was for her friends and colleagues to learn she was about to become Mrs. Don Juan. By the time the news got around to everyone, she'd probably be divorced. The thought of that sent a pain through her heart.

"You've changed."

He'd said that to her before. "I'm sorry."

"The hell you are!" He slammed down the phone.

She reached over to put the receiver on the hook, then lay back with a troubled sigh. It would have been better if she'd told him the truth tonight, that she'd decided to put acting behind her.

But she could only deal with one crisis at a time. Right now she wasn't in a fit state to handle D.L. who would be apoplectic when he heard the bad news.

All she could think about was Riley. Where was he tonight? Was he alone?

The phone rang again. Like before, the buzzer sounded. It was probably D.L. calling her back to rage a little more. If that was the case, then she would tell the truth and be done with it.

Once more she reached over to pick up the receiver. "D.L.?"

"No. It's Riley."

At the sound of his deep, rich voice her heart

pounded in her throat. "Where are you?" She knew she sounded like a hen-pecking wife, but she couldn't help it.

"I'm in Imola for the night."

Her hand tightened on the receiver. "Isn't that where you're going to race at the end of the month?"

"Yes. Since I haven't been on the racing circuit before, I had to get signed up so I can be in the qualifying test runs."

"I didn't know that."

"It's a formality I won't have to go through again. Tell me about your conversation with your agent. I assume he was calling you about another film."

"Yes," she murmured.

"I hope you told him you're going to be unavailable from here on out."

His arrogance was the last straw. "I haven't made a hard and fast decision about that yet."

"If that's the case, I'm calling off the wedding. Nicco just answered the phone so I know he's still up."

"Don't you dare call him, Riley!" she almost screamed into the phone. "I don't plan to make any more films, but I didn't want to get into that with D.L. tonight!"

"Why not?"

"Because they might be doing a sequel to the Cory Sieverts film, and there may be a clause in my contract on the first film that says I will be available if there's a second. I honestly don't remember."

"If there is, you'll have to break it."

"That could cost me all the money I've saved in the bank from my last film!"

"On Saturday you're going to become my wife. Any money problems we have will be my business."

"Just now you sounded like my father."

"Is that good or bad?"

She bit her lip, wishing she hadn't said anything. "He was the kind of man who saw his role as the protector and provider. He made my world so secure that when he died prematurely, I fell apart."

"Thus the reason you focused on a career that could bring you financial security."

"My mom had a hard time of it, Riley."

"I don't doubt it, but there are other jobs you could do that wouldn't require you to leave the country for weeks on end."

"What about you?" she cried out. "Racing forces you to travel from continent to continent on a monthly basis."

"I'm expecting you to travel with me so we're never apart. That's what marriage is all about."

Good marriages, Riley. Marriages based on love.

"You sound tired, sweetheart. I'm going to let you get to bed. The next time we see each other will be at the chapel. I don't dare come near you before then." His voice had fallen to another octave.

"The way I'm feeling right now, I want to make love to you until we're one pulsating entity, mindless of anything or anyone but each other. It's something I fantasized about too many nights in that hospital bed. The ache has become a need. Do you hear what I'm saying?"

Tears trickled down her cheeks. "Yes," she whispered, despising herself for loving a man who'd spoken words of physical need for her, nothing more.

* * *

The taxi was waved on through the grounds of one of the other royal palaces where Prince Enzo lived with his family and the elder Tescottis. When it drew up to a private side entrance, two uniformed guards stood ready to assist Riley and Mitra from the car.

She looked elegant bedecked with all her jewelry. A new black dress had been purchased for the occasion. She'd tied her favorite purple scarf around her head.

As she turned to him, there was a light in her dark eyes. "Before we go in, give me your hand."

They'd just come from the barge where other members of her family were making preparations for the wedding dinner. Riley smiled, wondering why she'd waited this long to read his palm, but he complied all the same.

To his surprise he felt her fold something warm and metallic into his palm. "A *baro manursh* gave this to me when I was a girl."

A *baro manursh* meant a great man. Riley wondered where this was leading.

"Everyone in the tribe recognized it as the symbol that we were to be married. But he became ill and whispered all his secrets to me before he died in my *tsara*."

It thrilled Riley to know she'd had a great romance in her life.

"Because of the money he left me, my family told me I didn't need to work. But I had a secret, too. In the tea leaves I'd seen a lost child wandering outside a tent. I saw clowns and balloons. It was the child he and I should have had. So I joined the circus."

Riley's throat started to swell.

"One day I heard a child crying and found this

beautiful little boy who was lost, clutching the string of a balloon in his hand. That day brought me great happiness.

"When you grew older, I was able to send you to my family where they made sure you were given the proper *Gadja* schooling. I would have gone home with you, but I didn't want your father to fear I had run off with you. Otherwise he would have taken you away from me much sooner."

Now Riley understood.

"Your father and I had many battles, but down here—" she pounded her breast, "he knew it was the right thing for you. His drinking was a sickness, but he always loved you. Do you know how I know that? Because he could have given you to strangers."

Every time Riley's father ran out of money, he went on one of his drinking binges and threatened to do just that. For years it put the fear in Riley until he got old enough to realize it was the alcohol that made his father say it.

"Today you make me proud by taking the step that will turn you into a *baro manursh*. You have earned the right to give this to your *Gadja* bride."

Before he even looked at it, Riley reached over and did something he'd always wanted to do as a grown-up. He kissed her on both cheeks, then rocked her in his arms.

"I love you, Mitra. My *Gadja* bride won't know the significance of this ring until tonight. But I can promise you that once she understands, she'll wear it with great pride and honor."

He finally let her go to examine the gold ring with the etching of a wild flower. She'd hidden it all these years.

Lifting his head he said, "Today I will honor you by having you sit at my side during the ceremony. That spot is normally reserved for the male parent of the groom, but I'm making an exception in your case."

"Why must I sit?"

He chuckled. "You can stand if you wish. I was afraid you might get too tired."

"I will stand. Now we must go in. I am curious to see if this woman is worthy of my *Gadja* child."

"How will you be able to tell?" he teased.

"There are ways," was all she said.

A quick glance at his watch told him they were late. The ceremony was scheduled for 11:00 a.m. It was already 11:10.

He climbed out of the car, then waved the guards aside while he helped her.

Riley had been here before to meet in private with the priest. Since this was Mitra's first time, he smiled to himself as he watched her look around at the opulence of the long mirrored gallery with its gilt moldings and white marble floor.

They passed through the gold gate to the inside of the exquisite chapel.

The Tescotti family had assembled around Father Luigi except for Nicco and Ann. They would come in when the organist started to play from the loft.

With various expressions of relief, the wedding party in all their finery watched Riley escort the Gypsy to the front of the chapel.

"Everyone? This is Mitra, the woman who raised me from the time I was two until I was seventeen. She's the only mother I've ever known. I've asked her to stand up for me today."

All the women's eyes filled with tears, but it was Callie's green orbs that drew Riley's attention.

He hadn't seen her in anything but a braid. Today she wore her hair down and looked particularly radiant in a cream-colored lace suit wearing a calla lily corsage. The same kind of yellow throated flower pinned to the lapel of his suit.

For a moment he could be forgiven for thinking Ann was standing there. Lord…in a few minutes, he was going to have his heart's desire.

The priest smiled at Mitra. "We're honored you could be here for this sacred occasion. If the two of you will stand to my left, we can begin."

The music had started. Outside the gold gate Ann shivered with fear and apprehension.

Riley was marrying her for the wrong reason. It wasn't the way a marriage was supposed to be. But the thought of hurting Nicco kept her silent.

Right now her brother-in-law was holding her hands to warm them. He looked stunning in his formal navy suit with a calla lily attached to his lapel.

"The last time I stood here, my bride was still slung over my shoulder wearing her jeans and sneakers. I have to tell you that for Riley's sake, I'm glad he's going to see a vision in white and orange blossoms as you walk to him willingly and eagerly."

"I'm sorry Callie cheated you out of that part, but I know something you don't."

His black eyes narrowed. "What?" he demanded. Anything to do with Callie and he became the intense, possessive husband her sister adored.

"She finally admitted to me that the evening she ran out of gas on your motorcycle, she could have ditched your bike much sooner and disappeared into the woods where you would never find her.

"But deep down, she wanted you to come after her because she'd already fallen in love with you. It was her plan to seduce you so Prince Enzo wouldn't want her anymore. According to her, *you* were the one who wouldn't cooperate in that department. That's why she went kicking and screaming to the altar."

Rich laughter poured out of Nicco. He crushed her in his arms. "Thank you for the belated wedding present. I owe you big time for that secret."

"Don't you dare tell her what I said."

"I swear she'll never know, but you've given me an idea for our first year anniversary coming up on Monday. Now let's go. Your husband-to-be has waited for you long enough."

He placed her hand on top of his left arm while a palace guard pushed the gate open for them. The walk to the altar began.

The moment she entered the chapel, Riley's gaze locked with hers. He looked impossibly handsome dressed in a formal light gray suit. Her heart flipped over and over as Nicco led her to his side.

She let out a soft gasp of surprise when Riley unexpectedly reached out and grasped her hand in a firm grip, pulling her close to him. Nicco let go of her to join Callie.

While she became lost in Riley's beautiful gray eyes, they swept over her from the crown of flowers in her hair to the tips of her white heels. The intimacy with which he studied everything in between created white-hot fire.

Faint from his devouring gaze, she finally looked

away to discover a pair of unfamiliar black eyes staring at her until she felt uncomfortable.

Standing next to Riley was a Gypsy woman in a purple scarf. Her stoic expression reminded Ann of Boiko's. She could be seventy or eighty. It was impossible to tell.

"Dearly Beloved, let us pray."

Father Luigi's voice reminded Ann they were in a sacred place and he was ready to proceed.

She averted her eyes and bowed her head. But throughout the prayer in Italian which she only partially understood, her mind was on the woman who'd played such an important role in Riley's life, he'd made her part of the ceremony.

The priest spoke in Latin during the marriage portion of the ritual.

When it came time for them to make their responses, Riley surprised her by answering in the same language he'd spoken to the little boy, Boiko.

She didn't understand any of it until he switched to English. "I, Riley Garrow, take thee, Annabelle Lassiter, for my lawfully wedded wife, and plight thee my troth with this ring that binds two souls into one mind, one heart, one belly."

The words were so unusual, Ann's breath caught.

She noticed the Gypsy woman nod as Riley placed a gold band on the ring finger of Ann's left hand.

Then the priest indicated it was Ann's turn.

She lifted her eyes to Riley, taking her cue from him. Though she didn't know the reason, she sensed on some deeper level how intrinsically important this part of the ceremony was for him. There was a vulnerability coming from him she hadn't thought pos-

sible. It frightened her that she might do something
wrong and ruin the moment.

"I, Annabelle Lassiter," she began in a tremulous
voice, "take thee, Riley Garrow, for my lawfully wedded husband, a-and accept this ring that binds two
souls into one heart, one mind, one belly."

An odd stillness seemed to surround Riley, yet his
eyes were alive with a silvery light. Whatever she'd
done appeared to have pleased him.

Ann quivered in relief before he said something in
an aside to the Gypsy whose gaze seemed to have the
ability to look straight into Ann's soul. Again the older
woman nodded.

"Since Annabelle and Riley have pledged their love
before God, family and friends, I hereby pronounce
them man and wife." Making the sign of the cross
Father Luigi said, "In the name of the Father, the Son
and Holy Ghost, Amen."

While Ann stood there waiting for the priest to tell
them they could kiss, he did the most extraordinary
thing and shook Riley's hand instead.

"Congratulations on your marriage," he said in
English. Then his gaze swerved to Ann. "I will be
happy to christen your baby when he or she arrives."

She frowned, still confused by the strange ending
to the ceremony. "We're not having a baby, Father."

Ann could hear Riley's chuckle over and above all
the others.

The priest put his palms together. "It is only a matter of time, my child."

Her face had probably gone as red as the bits of
color in the stained-glass windows forming the back-
drop of the beautiful shrine.

"Let's go," her new husband whispered. "We'll

have time to talk to everyone at the party.'' So saying, he grabbed her around the waist and rushed her down the aisle. She'd never seen any groom in such a great hurry to get away.

There were four palace limos waiting at the side entrance with police escorts. Riley climbed in the back of the first one. When a palace guard helped her inside and shut the door, Riley pulled her right onto his lap.

''What are you doing?'' she cried. He'd bent her over his arm so she couldn't move.

''If you'll stop asking questions, I'm going to give you that kiss you were waiting for.''

''Not here where everyone can see us, Riley!''

His voluble laughter rang throughout the limo interior. ''It's a much better place than inside the church where you would have been forced to control yourself. I happen to know what you're like when I get you in my arms.''

''You're terrible!''

''I know.''

As he lowered his head, she caught the glint of raw desire in his eyes. The thrill of it shook her to the core of her being. Then his mouth took over.

It had been a week since they'd been together like this. She moaned in pleasure. But it turned to pain when she realized his body was the only thing involved.

Those words he'd spoken during the ceremony about one mind and heart were a travesty.

Yet the way he was kissing her, she was having an impossible time denying him the belly part he wanted. That was because she wanted it, too.

CHAPTER SEVEN

THE limousine finally came to a stop, forcing Riley to relinquish her mouth. When the driver opened the door for them, Ann suffered shock as a series of camera flashes went off in succession. She buried her face against Riley's shoulder.

Nicco had warned her the paparazzi would rear their ugly heads. They always did when the royal family went out in public for an occasion like this. With their telephoto lenses, not even the police could control them.

What brought her fresh anguish was to realize she'd been caught looking totally ravished and disheveled by her new husband.

"My garland—where is it?" She was frantic.

"It just slipped to the side," Riley whispered. He kissed her swollen lips once more while he set it back in place. "There. Now you look like my blushing bride. Have I told you your beauty gave me heart failure when you entered the chapel today?"

"No," she grumbled. Ann wanted him to love her inner beauty.

"Don't be too upset I didn't kiss you in front of the priest."

"I *wasn't* upset."

"Liar," he muttered against the side of her neck. "A man doesn't show his passion for the woman at a Romany wedding ceremony. He must wait until the right time."

His mouth curved into a sensuous smile. "Out of deference to Mitra I waited as long as I could for me."

Falling more in love with him every second, she raised her blond head to search his eyes. "Who is Mitra?"

He sobered. "After you, the most important female in my life. She and her family have prepared our wedding feast. Now that everyone is aboard the barge, come with me and I'll introduce you."

Though a ladder had been set up to help people climb down into the barge from the pier, Riley called out to Nicco. "I want to carry my bride over the threshold the old fashioned way."

Her brother-in-law flashed them a smile before extending the plank to the shore. Riley gathered her in his arms and started across. Halfway there she felt him pause.

"What's wrong?"

"I need a kiss before I can take another step."

"Riley—you pick the absolute worst times!"

"Get used to it, Mrs. Garrow."

Mrs. Garrow. She couldn't believe it.

His mouth covered hers with smothering force. It was as if he was reminding her she belonged to him now and was staking his claim. In this mood Ann had no power to resist him.

He didn't set her down until they'd entered the cabin lounge where the families were chatting and enjoying themselves. With his arm hugging her waist, he led her to the chair where Mitra was seated. Ann could see that with her bone structure, she would have been a beautiful young woman.

"Ann? I'd like you to meet Mitra. She understands English much better than she pretends. I never knew my birthmother, but it didn't matter. Mitra became my mother. From the time I could toddle until I went to Russia with my father, she loved me as if I were her own. I'm not sure I would have survived without her.''

With those words, Ann's heart melted. Unable to help herself, she bent over and kissed the woman's cheek. ''I love you for loving Riley,'' she whispered against her ear so no one else could hear.

Mitra clapped her hands on either side of Ann's face, then whispered back in her ear, ''He will test your love in many ways. Be prepared.''

Test?

It was such a strange thing for her to say, Ann didn't know what to make of it. But the warning coming from the lips of a Gypsy made it sound prophetic.

An odd shiver chased down her spine.

Riley must have sensed something irregular because he pulled her back against him where she could feel his heart pounding.

''What are you two mumbling about?''

''That you're a challenge!'' Ann said the first thing to pop in her head. Anything to prevent him from learning the truth.

His laughter followed after her while she worked her way around the cabin exchanging hugs and kisses with all the families.

He hovered close by, then introduced her to Mitra's relatives. She'd brought two male and one female cousin who'd prepared all the food. When everything had been put out buffet style on the dining table, Riley announced they could start to eat.

Ann had never seen such a fabulous spread: beef, chicken, pheasant, fried potatoes, stuffed cabbage with rice, melon wedges and a kind of fruit cake drenched in brandy she couldn't get enough of.

"I saw you take a second helping of dessert," Callie murmured when they had a chance to be alone for a minute.

Riley had been summoned for a private conference with Nicco and Enzo. Maria had moved off the barge to say goodbye to the elder Tescottis.

"Don't tell me you're nervous to be alone with him after we all leave."

"Maybe I am a little."

Ann had never been intimate with a man and her sister knew it, but that wasn't what was tearing her apart.

"It's natural, but Riley's so much like Nicco, he'll put you at ease."

"I'm sure you're right."

"You can tell the man is painfully in love with you."

Ha!

Ann would give anything to be able to confide in Callie right now, but she didn't dare. Her sister always told Nicco everything. This was one time Ann had to keep quiet.

"Something else is wrong."

Oh, no.

"What is it, Ann? What did Mitra say to you?"

"She wished me well."

"If that's true, how come you looked so strange afterward?"

"Did I?"

"Stop pretending and talk to me!"

"All right! Sh-she intimated Riley could be difficult." It wasn't exactly what Mitra had said, but close enough.

Callie grinned. "Spoken like a true mother. Don't forget. She raised him and knows his greatness as well as his shortcomings."

If Riley had kept in touch with Mitra all these years, then she knew a lot more than that, like his proclivity for women and his need to drive himself to the edge at every opportunity...

What she'd let slip to Ann was only the tip of the iceberg. There were still many secrets to be uncovered.

No doubt she felt sorry for Ann knowing that Riley didn't love her. That's why she'd told her to be prepared.

Little did Mitra realize her *Gadja* child had already broken Ann's heart the night he'd coerced her into this mockery of a marriage.

"Don't look now but Nicco's making signals for me to leave with him. We both know Riley can't wait to get you to himself. You have the rest of today and tomorrow to forget the world and enjoy each other."

Callie squeezed her. "I'm so happy for you I can hardly stand it. When you come down to earth, call me."

"I promise."

They walked arm in arm through the cabin to the outer deck of the barge. Everyone had started to leave. While Mitra and her family climbed into one limousine, Enzo and Maria got into the other.

Pretty soon there was just Nicco and Riley. He stared at Callie, then Ann.

"You two are quite a sight," he said in a husky voice.

"I second that," Nicco followed.

Riley's eyes narrowed. "In all fairness to Colin Grimes, he didn't stand a chance."

Nicco grimaced. "Nevertheless it's long past time he started grousing in someone else's preserves."

"Nicco—" Callie sounded scandalized.

"He damn well better," Riley bit out.

Ann felt Callie give her a tiny pinch at the waist. Whether it was personal or professional, Riley could be as fierce as Nicco if he thought anyone was crowding his territory. In that respect, the two men could be scary.

Callie let go of Ann and walked toward her husband. In that moment, Ann started to panic. She wasn't ready to be alone with Riley yet. Suddenly now that they were man and wife facing the prospect of their honeymoon, it was the last thing she wanted.

"Since Bianca's keeping Anna for the rest of the day, shall we get changed and go for a ride?" she heard Nicco murmur.

Her sister rose on tiptoes to kiss him. "I'd love it." Nicco blew Ann a kiss, then climbed in the back of the limo with his wife.

A ride!

That was it!

Since Nicco believed the best wedding present she could give Riley was the news that she'd learned some basics of riding and was willing to fool around with him, why not bestow his gift right now?

If Riley were in love with her, she'd want to kidnap her husband for as long as she could get away with it. But he wasn't in love! In fact the sooner he possessed her, the sooner he'd get bored and want to be anywhere else except with her.

She couldn't stand that.

What if she were able to put him off for a while? Anything to delay the inevitable until they got to know each other better. Maybe by some miracle he'd learn to love her a little.

After waving them off, Riley moved toward her with a look in his eyes that set her heart pounding unmercifully. He cupped her face. "Dear Lord— I thought this moment would never come."

His lips roved over her features, sending fingers of delight through her system. "You have the most perfect mouth and eyes and hair I've ever seen. Father Luigi would tell me it's a sin to want you as much as I do, but I don't particularly care."

He began to kiss her. Slow sensual kisses that built in rhythm, melding their mouths and bodies, arms and legs. He lifted her in his arms and carried her inside the cabin to the bedroom. Their bedroom now.

The world spun. She felt the mattress against her back. Riley followed her down, then he was opening up another world to her she had no idea existed.

With each caress of his hands and mouth, he provoked a primitive response she was helpless to withhold. The intensity of her desire coursed through her like shock waves.

Intellectually she knew a man and woman were sexual beings, but she'd never been awakened to this side of her nature before.

This had to stop before she lost heart, soul, identity, will, everything he was capable of stealing from her.

"Riley—" she cried, wrenching her lips from his.

Passion glazed his eyes. "What is it, sweetheart?" His breathing sounded shallow. "Am I going too fast for you?"

She rolled her head back and forth. "It's not that,

but I was hoping to give you your wedding present first.''

He covered her throat with kisses. ''You're all the present I want.''

Afraid she'd waited too long she said, ''You wouldn't say that if you knew what it was.''

She felt a quickening in his body before he expelled his breath and rolled away from her.

He probably thought she wanted to retire to slip on a black lace nightgown she'd bought just for him. Whatever he thought it was, he'd be wrong. Yet she *had* caught his attention—enough for his curiosity to take hold.

''I won't be long.'' She kissed his lips, but when she would have darted from the bed, he pulled her back to devour her with a hunger that left her unsteady.

''I'm counting to ten.''

By the time she reached the bathroom, the dress he'd undone had fallen to the floor in a flimsy white pool. Her high heels and garland were somewhere on the floor between the lounge and the bed.

Thankful she hadn't had time to unpack her suitcase Nicco had brought over earlier, she slipped on some new tan jeans and a kelly-green cotton sweater. From her purse she pulled out the remote that opened the door to Nicco's private office. She slipped that in her pocket.

''What's taking you so long?'' he called to her from the bedroom.

Once she'd put on her new tan sneakers and hung up her dress on the bathroom door peg, she was ready. ''I'm coming.''

At this juncture Riley was standing by the bed, tying

the belt of his dark blue toweling robe. When he saw her in the doorway, his eyes did a double take. The look of shock on his handsome face was priceless.

"Oh! I should have told you to change into casual clothes," she said in an offhand manner. "Your present isn't on board. We'll have to drive to it."

He raked a hand through his black hair in what she recognized as a gesture of extreme frustration. It was kind of frightening and exciting to tease him like this.

"How did you plan to get to where we're going? The only form of transportation we have is my motorcycle which is locked up inside the engine room."

"I know. Since we don't have a car, I guess I'll have to ride on the back of it."

His black brows furrowed ominously. "What's going on, Ann?"

"Nothing," she answered in a quiet voice, injecting the slightest tone of despair. For effect, her eyes filled with tears. She was an actress after all, and had learned how to cry tears on demand. "I-it doesn't matter."

"The hell it doesn't!" he ground out. "If it's that important to you, then of course we'll go. But I happen to know motorcycles terrify you. Why don't you call for a taxi while I get dressed."

For Riley, he was being very sweet about this. Much sweeter than she would have been if the shoe were on the other foot. They'd only been married five hours, yet already she'd learned he could put her needs above his own. That was something important to find out about a husband, even if their marriage was only temporary she reminded herself.

"All right. I'll wait for you on shore."

So far, so good.

Ten minutes later Riley emerged from the cabin

wearing faded denims and a navy pullover. He looked fantastic in anything he wore. His gaze scanned the road leading down to the water.

"No taxi yet?"

"I—I decided not to call for it after all. It seems ridiculous when you have a perfectly good bike. If you'll promise not to go too fast, I'll try riding with you."

As he stood there staring at her, she could tell he didn't know what to think.

"You don't have to do this, Ann. I ride a bike for a living and don't expect my wife to share that interest. Whatever the reason for your fear, I respect it."

Every word that came out of his mouth made her love him a little more.

"I realize that, but I at least ought to be able to ride behind you if I have to. What if there were an emergency of some kind?"

His hands had gone to his hips in that male stance she loved. "Next week I intended on buying you a car for your wedding present. Now you've spoiled my surprise." But he smiled as he said it.

Oh, Riley—I love you so much you'll never know.

"I didn't mean to do that." She smiled back. "The thing is, I really do want to give you your gift now."

One brow lifted. "It's that good is it?"

"Yes." Convinced Nicco had known what he was talking about in the wedding present department she said, "As long as you'll be the one driving and can tell me exactly what to do, I'd like to try.

"Now that I'm married to a pro racer, I'd feel like a fool if someone found out Mrs. Riley Garrow had never even sat on the back of a bike."

Her comment brought a tinge of admiration to his

eyes. It shouldn't have thrilled her. She shouldn't care so much.

"Give me a minute and I'll bring it out." That was excitement she'd heard in his voice just now. A different kind of excitement than he'd displayed during their brief moment of rapture in the bedroom.

When he moved his bike out on deck, she noticed he was wearing his helmet and leather jacket. After firing it up, he drove across the plank in the Garrow inimitable style, then parked it in front of her. He climbed off exhibiting an eagerness that was unmistakable.

"You'll have to get used to wearing a helmet and jacket. These will have to do for now."

"What about you?"

His eyes smiled. "Unless this famous present is in Switzerland, I'm not concerned."

Ann chuckled. "Not quite. I—I hid it in a place you wouldn't think to look for it."

"Is that so." He stole a kiss from her astonished mouth. She'd captured his attention in a big way now.

"Yes," she came back breathlessly. "Nicco's private office."

He gave an incredulous shake of his dark head. "The plant is closed."

"No problem. Callie gave me her remote. So tell me what I have to do first."

"Let's put you in this."

He removed his jacket and helped her on with it. The warmth from his body heat enveloped her. But it was the feel of his hands sweeping her hair back that produced an almost erotic sensation before he lowered the helmet and fastened the chin strap. The shield was still up.

It was a good thing she'd had three full days of practice wearing the riding gear Nicco had picked out for her. They took some getting used to. Now she didn't think about it.

"How does it feel?"

"Confining."

The masculine hands resting on her shoulders kneaded them with gentle pressure. "Ann—at any point you're not comfortable with this, I'll have your promise that you'll tell me."

He was nervous.

Who would have guessed this mattered so much to him? More than ever she understood Nicco. When Callie stole his bike out from under him and took off, she really set her hooks in him.

"The plant's not that far from here. I'll be fine."

She noticed the way Riley's chest rose and fell. He was having a struggle with himself.

"When I get on the bike, you climb on behind me and put your feet on the pegs. Then slide your arms around my waist and hold on tight locking your fingers together."

Nicco had practiced this with her enough times she knew what to do.

"Okay."

"You lower your shield like this."

After he'd shown her, he straddled the bike, then helped her to get on. "How are you doing?"

It was sheer joy to flatten herself against his back. "Fine."

"There's time to change your mind."

"I won't."

"I swear I'll do everything in my power to protect

you," his voice throbbed. "You're a brave woman. Do you know that?"

If he thought that about her, then this whole exercise was worth it. She had a hunch a man like Riley would value courage above even physical beauty in a woman.

He started the motor. "Here we go."

His takeoff was so smooth, they seemed to glide right up the road of the embankment. Once they'd merged onto the main highway, he kept his speed with the flow of traffic and stayed in the right lane. Not once did he make any surprise moves that would frighten her.

Riley was being so careful with her, she wanted to cry. Instead, she pressed against him, enjoying the feel of his big hard body.

Too soon they reached the Danelli plant. Riley drove into the parking area and pulled around the side in front of Nicco's private door.

He came to a stop with the gentleness of a snow-flake landing on your cheek.

She climbed down and removed the helmet. He shut off the motor and set the stand before levering himself from the bike. Their eyes met and clung.

"You didn't panic once."

Ann could hardly breathe for the admiring expression in his soft gray gaze. "With Riley Garrow at the controls, why would I."

He crushed her in his arms. "I'm proud of you." They rocked back and forth for a minute.

There are more surprises in store for you, my love.

She kissed the edge of that firm male jaw before removing his jacket. "Come inside with me."

The remote undid the lock that allowed her to open

the door. He followed her down the hall to Nicco's suite. An adrenaline rush escalated her excitement.

"Wait here," she cautioned. "I'll be right back."

After putting his helmet and jacket on a chair, she walked through another door to the back room.

Her beautiful lavender and purple bike sat in the middle of the floor like a proud little lady. After riding it almost constantly for three days, she'd grown very attached to it.

Nicco had not only outfitted her with a lavender helmet, he'd given her a lavender and cream leather jacket, pants and gloves to match. Everything sat on the shelf.

It was his considered opinion that attractive colors reduced accidents because other drivers noticed you right away.

"Ann?"

His impatience delighted her.

"One more minute!"

Galvanized into action, she lifted the stand and walked her bike through to the office.

Riley was half-lounging against the edge of Nicco's desk. When she emerged from the back room with it, he took one look and straightened in shock.

"Do you like your present?"

"Sweetheart—" He sounded as if he didn't quite know how to couch his words. "You're a generous woman by nature, and I'm overwhelmed with your desire to please me. But I only need one bike, and it's outside."

Ann had never had so much fun in her life.

"This isn't everything."

He shook his head. "You're all that matters to me. I don't want gifts."

Oh, yes you do, Riley Garrow. You just don't know it yet.

"Indulge me a little longer?"

"Do I have a choice?" he whispered. Her brand-new husband sounded as if he'd reached the point where he couldn't take much more.

"No. I promise you're going to like it."

Spinning around, she hurried in the back room once more and donned all her riding gear, making certain to put the remote in her leather pocket.

When she entered the office the second time, she pretended she was a model on a walkway and paraded past him putting a wiggle in her step.

"As you'll notice ladies and gentlemen, this year Mr. Nicco Tescotti is showing the latest in his fall collection for the woman in the family who'll be looking smart as she roars to the supermarket on her new Danelli Supercharger."

Riley stood there so mesmerized, she didn't hear one peep out of him.

"This particular outfit was designed expressly for the wife of Mr. Riley Garrow, the latest racing sensation to come along in decades. To quote Mr. Tescotti, 'Mr. Garrow is the secret weapon in our arsenal.'

"In a twist on the tradition of the knights of old who wore their favorite lady's color, Mrs. Garrow will be sporting her knight's favorite color. It's her tribute to him while he breaks one speed record after another across Europe and elsewhere."

Satisfied with her performance, she reached for her bike. "Shall we go for a spin, Mr. Garrow?" she threw at him.

He didn't move. In fact he looked planted to the floor. Her joy was full.

"Would you mind opening the door for me?"

Like a sleepwalker, he finally did her bidding. She pushed her bike outside into the twilight.

He followed with his jacket and helmet in hand. His eyes had narrowed to silvery slits. "How long have you known how to ride?" his voice grated.

She pressed the remote to lock up, then slipped it inside her leather pocket. "Three days. Beat you home!"

"Ann— Stop!" He sounded terrified.

Bubbling with laughter, she started her bike and took off. Nicco and Callie had ridden enough with her in city traffic that she felt comfortable as long as she didn't do anything foolish.

Through the sideview mirror she could see a green-and-black motorcycle gaining on her. The traffic was light on a Saturday night. She increased her speed a couple of notches to stay ahead of him.

He was making ground fast and furiously, heedless of the speed limit postings. The thrill of the chase was upon her. She was determined to reach the barge first.

When he could see that she rode well enough for a novice, maybe she could talk him into taking a short ride in the mountains where they could enjoy a late dinner.

Anxious to put off the moment when they went to bed for the first time, she pushed faster, loving the way the bike leaped ahead, accelerating like magic at her touch. For the first time she could understand what all the excitement was about.

You could go anywhere on one of these things in half the time it took everyone else. In the freedom of the open road, the weight of the world left you and you felt you had wings.

Euphoric over her plans thus far, she turned at the light and came to the private road that led down to the embankment. Riley was almost upon her now.

On an enormous high, she wanted to impress him. If he could cross the plank without problem, so could she. But she'd underestimated her speed. When she applied the rear brake with her right foot, the bike slid. She turned the handlebars to make the correction, not realizing the brake had locked up. In the next instant she found herself tipping sideways into the shallow water.

Her surprised cry was joined by a yelp from Riley who'd plunged in after her. With Herculean strength he lifted her into the barge and removed her helmet.

"Are you all right?" he cried frantically.

She nodded between coughs from the water. "I—I'm fine. D-do you think I broke my new b-bike?"

"Forget the damn bike!" he bit out before she heard him swear a string of invective several blocks long.

"What in heaven's name possessed you to try anything so dangerous?" By now she was cradled in his arms. She felt his hands travel everywhere examining her for injuries. He had no idea what his touch was doing to her.

Ann had no idea he could tremble so hard. She felt it resonate to the depth of her being.

"I wanted to show you I could ride as well as Callie. Now I understand what they say about pride."

He pressed his forehead against hers. "Don't ever do that to me again."

"I'm fine, Riley. If you want to know the truth, I feel perfectly stupid."

"It was a stupid thing to do," he raged, but it didn't have quite the fierce anger to back it up this time.

"I know. I promise I'll never do anything that dumb again."

"Lord, how I wish I believed that."

He sounded like he'd been in the accident!

"I hate to ask anything more of you, but do you think you could check my bike over and see if it's badly damaged?"

"First we're going to get you out of all these wet clothes."

Oh, no!

She eased away from him and got to her feet with about as much grace as a hippo rising from the mud.

"A little water never hurt anyone." She looked at her bike. Without wasting another second, she slipped over the side. The water was only a couple of feet deep. She grabbed the handlebars and set it upright. "Hey—it looks like it might be okay."

Another curse word escaped as Riley stormed in after her and walked the bike to the shore. She followed him, then hunkered down to examine it for any damage.

"Your rearview mirror's broken," he said after a few minutes.

"If that's all you can find wrong, then I got off scot-free."

His jaw hardened. "Don't assume your next accident will have the same outcome."

"I'll practice riding across that plank until I get it perfect."

His eyes flared an angry gray. "The hell you will."

She smiled at him. "You know something, Riley. You swear too much."

He started to swear again, then caught himself.

"Thank you for saving me." She kissed the end of his nose. "I'm married to a real live hero."

CHAPTER EIGHT

RILEY was right about the aches and pains. By the time she'd taken her shower and hung up her leathers to dry, her nightgown-clad body felt battered as she slid between the sheets.

Though there wasn't a mark on her yet, she imagined by morning there'd be a few bruises along her right forearm and thigh where she was tender. Without all the protection Nicco had insisted she wear, she could have cut herself up pretty badly on the rocks along the river bed.

She was lucky the bike hadn't fallen on top of her, or she'd probably be nursing a broken arm or leg.

No sign of Riley yet. She could hear his footsteps as he moved around the barge getting everything ready for the night.

If she hadn't had the accident, they might be in the mountains by now ordering a delicious meal at some charming inn. Instead she'd achieved the one thing she'd hoped to prolong. She was in bed exactly where Riley wanted her.

"I warmed some soup for you," a voice sounded in the semidarkness.

"Thank you," she said with her heart in her throat.

"Can you sit up, or do you want me to help you?"

He'd just thrown her a life preserver.

"I—I'm pretty sore."

Riley moved around to her side and turned on the lamp before sitting down on the edge of the bed. He

137

put the tray with the soup and crackers on the end table.

Her pleading green eyes sought his above the sheet she'd pulled to her neck. "Have you forgiven me yet?"

Shadows had darkened his features making him look older. Yet grim or smiling, he was the most gorgeous man on earth. "You came close to giving me a heart attack today."

"I'm sorry our marriage has already aged you," she teased to lighten his gloomy mood.

He fed her several spoonfuls of vegetable beef soup. It tasted good. "Three days of expert training from a pro like Nicco still doesn't prepare you to take the kind of risk that sent you hurling down the embankment."

"I swear that will never happen again, Riley. It's just tha—"

"I know," he interrupted her in a grave tone. "You wanted to make me happy."

"A-are you?" her voice caught.

He eyed her with an unfathomable expression.

Uh-oh. Maybe Nicco had figured wrong this time. "There are a lot of men who like to do guy things with guys. If the idea of riding around with your wife turns you off, just say so."

He grimaced before feeding her some more soup. "You know that's not the case."

"Then I don't understand."

"I don't want you doing something to please me for the wrong reason."

Ann blinked in confusion. "But I *want* to please you. What's wrong with that?"

He reached out to smooth a damp blond tendril from

her temple. Her body felt his soft touch like a current of electricity. "Have you always competed with your sister?"

She jerked to a sitting position, pulling the bedspread with her. "Is *that* what you think I do?" she demanded. His question hurt her more than he would ever know.

"I have news for you, Rocket Man," she lashed out. "When I asked Nicco what he thought you'd like for a wedding present, he said I should learn to ride. In fact he told me I owed it to my famous husband to try. It was all *his* idea. If you don't believe me, ask him!

"Naturally I have my pride and would like to think that in time I could become as good a cyclist as Callie, but I realize that will take years. If I weren't married to you, the thought of learning how to ride would never have occurred to me.

"You're the one who coerced me into marrying you. Nicco was just as bad by forcing me to get on a bike. If it weren't for the two of you, we wouldn't be having this absurd conversation because there wouldn't be any *us!*"

Scrambling to the other side of the bed, she pulled the quilt around her and stalked out of the room. No doubt she'd pay for her hasty retreat come morning.

"Where in the hell do you think you're going?"

"To get some sleep. And by the way, you're swearing again!"

Heartsick, she staggered into the lounge and lay down on the couch. At this rate their marriage wasn't going to last twelve hours!

When she felt his hand on her wet cheek, she buried her face in the cushion.

"Ann?" he whispered in a husky voice. "I should never have said what I did about you and Callie." His tone was filled with self-recrimination. "Don't you know I only threw that at you because I was so terrified to watch you lose control? Anything could have happened to you."

She flung around. "Now maybe you know how I feel at the thought of you crashing with another cyclist going two hundred miles an hour."

His hand gripped her arm. "From the time I was old enough to watch my father ride through fire, I knew that kind of fear. Every time he did a stunt, I wondered if it would be his last and I'd never see him again. That's when I'd go running to Mitra's wagon.

"If she was reading tea leaves for the circus crowd, I'd sit in her favorite rocking chair and eat cookies she made and kept in a special jar just for me. When she came home, she'd tell me stories about her past or take me for walks. Her comforting presence kept my fears at bay."

"Thank heaven for her!"

"I have. Many times. If my father was drunk, then he didn't come for me. I loved it on those nights. She'd put me to bed in satin sheets and sing songs until I fell asleep. But when I wasn't with her, I had terrible nightmares. Oddly enough they were about the mother I couldn't remember."

Hot tears squeezed out from under Ann's lashes.

"That's why they were so terrible. In my child's mind, every little boy had to have a mother. But she didn't want me. My father married two other women hoping to find me one, but being a mother wasn't their first or last priority."

Her heart bled for the boy in the man. "Did you ever meet her?"

"No, and to this day I have no idea if she's dead or alive. Mitra told me it was better I didn't know. That was good enough for me.

"When I turned seventeen, my father told me we were leaving for Russia. I think the only reason we left was because he feared Mitra's power over me. For many years she'd paid for me to go to school in Perugia where her relatives lived.

"I'd come home on holidays and in the summer. But each time I returned I noticed my father's alcoholism was worse. No doubt he had visions of me abandoning him like my mother did.

"Before we left on the train, Mitra sat me down and explained that he was blessed with good looks but no sense about women. She warned me I must find a woman who respected herself above all else, otherwise I would end up exactly like him.

"That put the fear in me because by then all I could think about were beautiful girls and motorcycles.

"Twelve years later when I met you on the set and you cut me dead, I was reminded of Mitra's warning. For the first time since I'd left her influence, it struck me I'd come across the kind of woman of whom she could approve."

"So that's why you married me? Because of what Mitra said?"

"Yes, plus the fact that Sister Francesca told me it was time I settled down with a good woman.

"I knew you were good when I saw you take compassion on Boiko. The *Gadjas* I've known don't understand Romanies, they keep away and certainly don't kiss one."

Ann was stunned.

Riley Garrow had to be the most exasperating, complicated, frustrating, unorthodox, exciting, amazing, remarkable man she'd ever known. Being raised by Mitra explained a lot about his nature.

He will test your love in many ways. Be prepared.

Riley's unhappy childhood had robbed him of the capacity to love, to believe in it. That's what Mitra had tried to tell Ann.

Knowing Riley had chosen his bride according to some criteria she'd passed without even realizing it, placed the reason for his marriage proposal in a completely different light for Ann.

"Forgive me if I overreacted to your accident. I'm afraid it brought back my old fears. Now come to bed."

He kissed her neck. "I promise I won't do anything you don't want me to. But I hope you'll let me hold you. After the scare you gave me, I need to feel you against me for the rest of the night."

When he picked her up and took her back to the bedroom, she didn't have the power or desire to resist. There was no conversation as he got her settled, then left to shower.

While Ann waited for him to join her, she took off her wedding ring and studied the wild flower etching in the lamp light.

In a few minutes Riley slid under the covers wearing the robe she'd seen him in earlier.

She turned to him. "This is no ordinary ring."

"Mitra's fiancé was a wealthy Gypsy. He died before they could be married, but he left her everything. That's how she was able to take care of my expenses when my father was down and out. I didn't know she had this ring until she gave it to me outside the palace this morning.''

"I feel very honored to wear it."

Riley took it from her and pushed it home on her ring finger. "It's a perfect fit. I have another ring for you, but I'll wait until a special occasion to give it to you."

He reached across her to turn off the lamp. "Since I don't know where you hurt, I'm going to let you figure out how we're going to do this."

With an eagerness that was embarrassing, she drew his right arm beneath her head, then turned on her left side. With her arm wrapped around his chest, she buried her face in his neck.

He gathered her tightly against him, engulfing her in his male warmth.

Oh…he felt so good.

"Does your mouth hurt?"

"No."

"Then I'd like a taste of it."

Obeying a compulsion stronger than her will, she moved her face against his smooth shaven jaw until their mouths fused in passion. Tonight the pleasure of kissing each other into oblivion dulled the pain of knowing he hadn't married her for love.

Monday morning Riley rode his wife's bike up to one of the bay doors of the Danelli garage and rang the buzzer. As soon as it lifted, he drove on through to find a free slot where it could be worked on. All the mechanics who were on board nodded to him and called out their congratulations.

In-house gossip had already spread the news that he'd married the sister of the boss's wife. The bridal picture on the front page of Turin's Sunday newspaper had done the rest. Some photographer had managed to catch Riley carrying Ann to the barge where the royal family was looking on.

The caption read, Hollywood Film Star And Danelli Racing Idol Wed At Tescotti Palace. The Romantic Duo Will Spend Their Honeymoon Cruising The Po.''

The staff writer had gotten the "wed" part right. As for the honeymoon, that was a different story.

So far his bride of two days was still inviolate due to injuries suffered in a biking mishap.

His jaw clenched.

That was about as far as Riley could stomach reading while he stood in line at a service station to pay for some oil. He'd waited until this morning to start up her bike. It had fired, but it wasn't running the way it should. He'd decided to add oil to the fuel as a precaution before he reached the plant.

Carlo, one of the younger mechanics, walked over to him. "What seems to be the trouble, Signore Garrow?"

"The engine has suffered water damage," Riley explained without going into details.

"Looks like it needs a new mirror, too."

Riley nodded. "See what you can do, will you?"

"I'll run it through some tests right now."

"Thanks, Carlo. I'll be in the boss's office if you need me."

A few minutes later he'd walked through the main plant to the other building that housed Nicco's office.

He found his new brother-in-law busy at the computer. When Nicco spotted him in the doorway, he looked up in surprise.

"I thought I told you to take the rest of the week off to enjoy your honeymoon."

"I might have done if my bride hadn't gotten it in her head to present me with her wedding present as soon as our guests left the barge. I'm here to pay for it."

"That was my gift to her." Nicco sat back in his swivel chair with a big grin on his face. "I noticed it was missing from the back room this morning. So how did you like it?"

Riley sucked in his breath. "For starters, it added about twenty years to my life."

"What else?" Nicco was a quick study. He sat forward, no longer smiling.

"Let's just say that due to my bride's incapacitation, the honeymoon hasn't started yet."

Some of the color left Nicco's face. "How bad is she?"

"She hasn't broken any bones, thank God, but she's sustained some serious bruising on her right arm and leg."

"Tell me what happened."

Riley related the facts. "When I saw her go flying down that embankment, I swear my whole life flashed before me."

By now Nicco was on his feet. "She swore to me she'd never take any unnecessary risks. I was wrong to bully her about getting on a bike. If she was frightened of them before, this has killed any hope of her overcoming her phobia. Callie's going to be crushed when I tell her."

"Don't beat yourself up, Nicco. To Ann's credit she did everything right until she reached the marina. Let's both be honest. In our early biking days we probably would have underestimated the steepness of the road, too.''

''I'm sure that's true, but I wasn't on my honeymoon at the time. It's my fault yours was ruined.''

''No it's not. The only thing of any importance is that she's going to be all right. I'm married to the woman I want. When the honeymoon starts is immaterial. If anything, it has opened my eyes.''

''You mean you found out the real meaning of fear when you thought you might have lost her?''

''Yes,'' Riley admitted in a tortured whisper. ''If she feels that same fear every time I suit up for a race, I don't give our marriage a chance in hell. There's something else you should know. Something I'm not proud of.''

''Go on.''

''Ann didn't want to marry me, but I applied certain leverage that made it impossible for her to deny me.'' In a few minutes he'd put Nicco in the picture. ''The bottom line is, she'd do anything for you, or to keep you from being hurt. I'm afraid I'm not a nice man.''

''That makes two of us,'' Nicco confessed. ''Callie did everything but poison me to prevent our marriage from taking place. At least you didn't have to use brute force to get Ann to the altar.''

Riley stared at him. ''You forced your marriage to help your brother. My reasons for coercing Ann were totally selfish.''

''Don't give me any credit,'' Nicco bit out. ''I wanted Callie the second I saw her get off the plane. Once she flashed those green eyes at me, that was it!''

''I had the same reaction when Ann and I met on the set,'' Riley muttered.

''Your marriage to her is more important than any

racing career. If you hadn't seen that magazine article and come to Turin, the Danelli company would still continue to grow. Not with the kind of excitement the legendary Riley Garrow could bring to it of course." Nicco smiled. "Maybe fate has something else in store for you."

Riley's senses went on full alert. He knew Nicco well enough to realize the man didn't make comments like that without a reason.

"What do you know I don't?"

"While Enzo and I were on the barge talking, he told me he wanted to have a private chat with you after your honeymoon. Since Ann is still recuperating, maybe this week would be the best time to accommodate him."

Riley frowned. "Why would he want to see me?"

"If you think I've engineered anything, you'd be mistaken. After guiding Ann in the wrong direction about her choice of wedding present for you, I'm through meddling in your affairs, even if it was with the best of intentions."

"I know that," Riley assured him. Nicco Tescotti was the best of the best.

"Enzo was talking as the prince, not as my brother. If it were a social call, he'd have left it up to Maria to issue an invitation to you and Ann."

Riley rubbed his chest absently. "If his schedule isn't too full, I could see him today. Callie drove her car over to the barge to take Ann home with her for part of the day."

"Good. I'll give Enzo a call on his private line now." He pulled his cell phone out of his pocket. After he punched the digits he said, "Is the bike totalled?"

"No. I rode it in, but it has problems. Carlo's looking it over. My purpose in coming in here was to settle the bill with you." He pulled his credit card out of his wallet.

"Put it away. I told you Callie and I gave it to her. As it turns out, it was the wrong thing to do. If it can be salvaged, we'll use it as a demonst— Enzo?" he greeted his brother.

"I'm glad I caught you. I've got Riley here. It seems they're not leaving on their honeymoon yet, so he's available." After a moment his gaze flicked to Riley. "Can you meet at the palace at eleven-thirty for lunch?"

"Of course."

"He'll be there. I'll drive him over. *Ciao, fratello.*"

One of the drawing rooms of the palace had been converted into an office for Callie to run the business of the preserve. While her sister was needed in the surgery, Ann sat down at the computer. Since Riley felt it was important to see about her bike, today was the perfect time to look for a job on-line. She was too sore to do anything more than sit or lie down.

Since her accident he'd treated her like a princess. There didn't seem to be enough he could do for her. She had no idea he was such a wonderful cook and nurse. Out of consideration for her injuries, he'd been careful how he'd held her both nights. There'd been no question of his trying to make love to her.

Being the contrary soul she was, she found herself wanting much more than the affectionate kisses he gave her when he brought her something to eat or read.

On Sunday he kept busy cleaning the barge. Toward

evening he fished off the bow while she lay in a lounger to watch.

Earlier this morning after breakfast, he'd announced he was leaving for the plant with her bike. That is if he could get it running. She'd held her breath waiting to hear if the engine would start. When it did, she sighed with relief. For such a beautiful piece of engineering to be drowned within ten minutes of leaving the shop wasn't to be tolerated.

Once he was out of sight, she'd called Callie to ask if she could come over. After hearing the details of the accident, her sister had been uncharacteristically silent. Then she'd changed the subject and said she would drive to the marina to pick her up.

"You've been at this for hours!" Callie exclaimed. She swept into the office with two tall glasses of iced tea for them. "Found anything interesting yet?" She sat down next to her and handed her one.

"Thanks for the drink. Well, there are a few colleges around Italy that hire American teachers with English degrees, but none of them are in Turin."

"What about drama schools?"

"They want native Italians. Maybe if I advertised in the paper, I could be an English tutor for some Italian aristocrat's children."

"It wouldn't work. They'd want you to live in. I can just imagine how your husband would react to that."

So could Ann.

"He wants me to give up acting." Which was a mild way of putting it.

Callie eyed her in surprise. "I thought you'd decided not to do any more films."

"I may have to do one more if it's written in my

contract. D.L. will let me know,'' her voice trailed. She wasn't looking forward to his phone call if he had bad news for her. "I need to find an exciting new career where I can use my English degree.''

"I thought being Riley's wife filled those requirements,'' she teased gently.

"Not when he's off racing.''

After a long pause, ''Why don't we work out a deal? You could help me stay on top of preservation business. Anna keeps me so busy, I can't get to all of it as it is.''

"Thanks, Callie, but that's your area of expertise.''

Riley's question about her being in competition with Callie still bothered her. Even though he'd apologized for flinging that at her out of sheer frustration, she could understand why he might have thought it.

Though she'd never been jealous of Callie in any way, since meeting Riley, Ann did envy the closeness her sister and Nicco shared through their love of cycling.

In that regard Ann was determined that one day she'd be as good a rider as Callie. It might be the only way to hold on to Riley so he wouldn't get bored of her and ask for a divorce.

Thinking of her husband, she checked her watch. "It's after four. I'd better get back to the barge.''

"I'll drive you. Let me ask Bianca if she'll keep an eye on Anna.''

"Can I borrow your newspaper? I'm going to check the work ads.''

"You can have it. Nicco read it before he left for the office. I'll bring it out to the car on my way.''

After her sister left the room Ann drained the rest of her iced tea, then turned off the computer.

Today was only the first day of her job hunt. It might take several weeks, but before long she intended to be employed doing something that occupied her thoughts so completely, she wouldn't be able to dwell on her sham of a marriage.

To her surprise they passed Nicco on the way to the marina. "Darling," she heard her sister whisper under her breath.

Callie was as bad as Ann in the husband worship department. He was driving a Danelli company vehicle. Riley sat in the front passenger seat. His masculine appeal was so potent, Ann could hardly breathe.

Through the rearview mirror she watched her good-looking brother-in-law make a U-turn and follow them. Even if Nicco was driving, it was like déjà vu being chased by Ann's husband. Of course this time it was Callie at the wheel. Her car wouldn't go flying into the water.

Who knew what conclusions the two brothers-in-law had come to in private? She started getting nervous about the prospect of being alone with Riley. When her sister brought the car to a stop, Ann grasped her arm. "Stay for dinner. Please? We've got chicken and rice left over from the wedding."

"We wouldn't dream of it. Technically speaking you're still on your honeymoon. Don't look now but your husband is making a beeline for you. The man wants you all to himself."

Ann shook her head. "You wouldn't be interrupting anything. Believe me."

Her sister shot her a horrified glance, but before Ann could explain, the door flew open. Riley lowered his head and pressed a hard, swift kiss to her lips. "How are you feeling?"

"Fine," came her breathless answer.

Callie flashed her a secret smile as he helped her out of the car.

"Nicco says he'll meet you home, Callie. Thanks for looking after my wife."

"You're welcome. Ann? Don't forget your newspaper."

"Oh—"

Riley grabbed it and shut the door. "Why didn't you phone me?" he murmured against her hot cheek. "I would have brought you one home."

"I didn't think of it until the last second."

"What's so important?" He started to help her across the plank to the barge.

"I'm looking for a job and hoped to find one in the want ads."

An awkward silence followed. By the time they'd entered the cabin, both cars were out of sight. He trailed her into the lounge and tossed the paper on the coffee table.

The mention of the job had made him angry. She decided to change the subject. "What's the verdict on my bike?"

"You were born under a lucky star. Carlo said he'll have it running like new by tomorrow."

"That's a huge relief." She took a fortifying breath. "Was Nicco furious?"

"With himself maybe."

"What do you mean?"

His lips thinned. "I think you'd better sit down."

"Why?" she cried out in alarm.

"Because we have a lot to talk about and you're still recovering from a nasty accident."

"I'm doing much better."

He grasped her hands. When he kissed the tips, darts of awareness arced through her body. "I noticed you seemed steadier when you walked, thank God."

One minute he ran cold, then hot. She couldn't take his fire and ice treatment much longer. It was sending her over the edge.

His luminescent gray eyes studied her between heavy black lashes. "You need to know I leveled with Nicco today."

When the words sank in, her world tilted. She got this terrible pain in her chest. "H-how much did you tell him?"

He traced the line of her lips with an index finger. "Everything."

Liquid filled her eyes. "Why?"

Riley slid his hands to her neck. "He blamed himself for your accident. I couldn't let him do that."

She jerked away from him, white-faced. "Did you tell him you've decided not to race for his company after all?"

"Let's just say that certain unexpected factors have caused us to leave the matter open for further discussion."

"I can't believe you betrayed me like this." Tears started to trickle down her cheeks. "You knew how much I didn't want to hurt Nicco, but that didn't matter to you. He treated you like a brother. Look how you've returned his goodness. Nicco's worth a million of you!"

"Ann—"

"We got married for nothing!" Her hands had formed fists. "What kind of selfish game have you been playing? You may be one of the best looking men in existence, but you don't have the faintest clue what it takes to be a husband.

"I told you I didn't want to marry you, but you made certain it happened in the palace chapel itself with the royal family there to support you.

"One heart, one mind, one belly. What kind of a sick joke was that?"

His eyes had grown bleak. "You haven't given me a chance to finish telling you everything."

"You've said enough to convince me you're an amoral man. Knowing you broke my trust, how can you even stand here on this barge? Nicco gave it to you out of the generosity of his soul!

"You know what? Despite the fact that I'm divorcing you, I'm going to keep this ring in honor of Mitra who warned me about you."

His beautiful olive skin turned ashen.

"Every time I look at it, I'll be reminded that Riley Garrow, the prince of hearts, *has* no heart."

CHAPTER NINE

"HI, D.L."

He looked up from his desk. His thick red brows lifted in shock. "Good grief? Where did you come from? I just saw your picture in the newspaper. You and Garrow pulled the stunt of the year!"

"That's what it was."

"What do you mean?"

Ann plunked herself down on the chair opposite his desk. "It was a publicity stunt. You told me I needed to keep my face before the public."

He let out his loud laugh. "Are you fooling me?"

"Would I do that?"

"You mean you didn't get married and honeymoon on the royal yacht?"

"It was a barge, and there was no honeymoon. I'm here to find out if that sequel is going through." *And to pay a visit to my attorney.*

"I haven't heard yet. That's why I didn't call you."

"Tell me the truth. Am I tied to the fine print in the contract about a second film?"

He eyed her for a moment. "No."

"Okay. Now I know where I stand. Just so you're aware, I'm back at my condo."

She'd been lucky to have one to come home to. When she'd flown to Italy, she hadn't known she was going to be married, so she hadn't made any arrangements about her place or her furniture.

155

"D.L.? Do you think you could send me on some auditions that won't compromise my principles?"

He squinted at her. "Are you willing to do a voice for an animated classic feature film of *The Princess and the Pea?* The pay's not that bad."

The idea had never occurred to her, but it appealed more than anything else she could think of right now.

"Yes! I'd love it!"

"All right. I'll make the arrangements. You show up at the Briarwood studio tomorrow morning at 8:00 a.m. sharp."

Good. She needed work.

"Why don't you tell me about my part over dinner. I owe you."

"You're on, honey."

Relieved she was off the hook contract wise, she enjoyed her meal with him. He caught her up on all the latest gossip which prevented her from thinking. After they parted company, she went back to her condo.

The red light on the phone base was blinking. She could have checked the caller ID, yet it was the last thing she wanted to do.

The only person who knew she was back in Hollywood was D.L. But she had a feeling it was Callie. No doubt when she'd tried to reach Ann on the barge, Riley had been forced to tell her Ann had packed her bags and left the marina in a taxi.

That had been eighteen hours ago. Ann wasn't up to a talk with her sister yet.

She'd never cried so much in her life. Exhausted physically and emotionally, she got into bed and pulled the pillow over her head. When the alarm on her watch went off at six the next morning, she was thankful she'd been able to sleep that long without dreaming.

A half hour later she was showered and dressed in her red blazer style suit and white blouse. When she tied her hair back with a white scarf, it gave her a professional look with a flare. She needed that job!

But when she opened the door of her condo, her conscience wouldn't allow her to leave until she'd at least checked the Caller ID.

There were out of area calls plus others.

It would be three-thirty in the afternoon in Turin. This was the time Anna took her nap. Most likely Callie was at her desk in the office.

Realizing that if she were in her sister's shoes she'd be frantic by now, Ann phoned their private number at the palace. It rang twice before Callie answered in Italian. When she said hello, Ann cried, "Callie?"

"Hi! After the way Riley hustled you onto the barge Monday afternoon, I'm surprised he let you come up for air this soon," she teased.

Her eyes closed tightly. *Riley hadn't said a word to them.* That meant either he was still living on the barge, or he'd left Turin expecting Ann to inform the family of their breakup.

It shouldn't have surprised her but it did.

Once we're married the fire will burn itself out. It always does. Ask my father whose passion drove him to marry on three separate occasions. One by one they disappeared when the excitement was over.

"H-how's everything?" she stammered.

"The way it was two days ago. Ann—you sound funny."

"So do you. Maybe it's our connection."

"The connection has nothing to do with it. I'm getting strong vibes something's wrong."

Ann had made the mistake of calling. Now she had no choice but to tell her sister the truth.

"I'm in L.A."

Callie let out a surprised cry. "I can't believe it! You mean you really do have to make that film right now?"

"No."

"Oh, I get it. You and Riley decided to enjoy a honeymoon over there and see about your condo at the same time."

"He's not with me."

Silence ensued. Then, "Why not?"

"I—I'm getting an annulment."

"Annulment— You and Riley? That's impossible!"

"I'm surprised Nicco hasn't said anything to you yet."

"You mean you told my husband instead of me?" The mixture of incredulity and pain in her sister's voice started the tears all over again.

"No. I'm afraid Riley was the one to do that." She dashed the moisture from her cheeks. "I can't talk anymore or I'll be late for an audition. I promise I'll get in touch with you later."

"Ann—"

With her sister's cry still ringing in her ear, she hung up the phone and hurried out of her condo to hail a taxi.

After informing the receptionist at the studio that D.L. had sent her, she was told to go through the doors to her left, then down the hall and around to the first room on her right.

Ann thanked her, then proceeded to her destination,

but she never reached the turn because a tall, powerful looking man in a brown polo shirt and tan chinos came out of another room and blocked her path. He lifted his head in her direction.

Riley—

Her legs started to buckle. She fell against the wall for support so she wouldn't fall.

"It's nice to see you, too," he murmured silkily. "I'm surprised you didn't notice me on the plane seated a few rows behind you."

What?

"Uh-uh." He cupped her jaw with his hand. "Don't make a scene." He brushed his lips against hers in a feathery-light touch.

"You're going to go outside with me and get in my rental car. If you scream, all you'll manage to do is bring a lot of embarrassing attention to yourself.

"The woman in reception knows you're my wife and will realize we're having one of those celebrity domestic squabbles. Since our marriage is big news around Hollywood at the moment, the media will eat it up.

"So what's it going to be, Mrs. Garrow? Do you come quietly, or will I have to put you in a fireman's lift? I've done it before and won't hesitate to do it again."

Her heart skidded out of control. Damn damn damn him for his tenacious hold on her. "You're a devil!" she muttered under her breath.

His dazzling smile made a mockery of her anger. "A lot of women have told me that before. I had hoped my wife would have come up with something a little more original, but I must admit I've never been

called a prince with no heart before. The prince part
gives it a certain ring I find to my liking."

Two people came through the double doors and
walked between them. She noticed they turned around
twice to stare before they disappeared around the corner.

"What do you want?" she asked in a dull voice.
For the moment all the fight seemed to have gone out
of her.

"To have a sensible conversation with you."

"That isn't possible."

"When one person does all the talking, then I
agree."

"If you're trying to make me feel guilty, it won't
work, Riley. The loss of trust can't be regained. There
are some things you can't forgive," she whispered.

"Sister Francesca has a little different take on it. 'I,
the Lord God, shall forgive whom I will, but thou art
commanded to forgive all men their trespasses.'"

She lowered her head. "Why did she give *you* that
lecture?" Ann asked helplessly. Riley knew how to
get to her in such insidious ways, she was terrified.

"Sister Francesca was a psychiatric nurse as well
as a saint."

Her body quaked.

"You were put in a psychiatric ward after your accident?" her voice throbbed.

"It sounds scarier than it was. When my father's
best friend Bart came back again and again to try to
see me, I warned her to keep him away, or else."

Ann shuddered.

"She warned me that the hate and bitterness I felt
toward my parent was destroying my soul. I knew it

was the truth, but so help me at that point in time I didn't give a damn and told her to get out!

"Like the proverbial bad penny, she came back to sit at my side night after night while I raged against God, nature, all mankind. Especially *you.*"

Aghast that her rejection had played any part in his torment, she reeled in fresh pain.

"When I was too exhausted to rage anymore, she told me I had a visitor. It was Bart. Good old faithful, loyal Bart. My father's friend to the end. I'm sure Sister Francesca put him in the picture because we didn't talk about him.

"By the time I was released, I was able to give him a hug, but I still hadn't forgiven my father. That didn't come until the day of our wedding. Mitra said one thing that turned me around."

Ann should have cut this off five minutes ago, but Riley had a captive audience and he knew it. "What was that?"

"Your father's drinking was a sickness, but he always loved you. Do you know how I know that? Because he never abandoned you."

The breath Ann had held locked in her lungs escaped. "For your sake I'm glad you've resolved that much of your past, but none of this has to do with us."

Forgetting her appointment for the audition, she dashed for the double doors and hurried out of the studio into a barrage of camera flashes. When she turned to run back inside for cover, she came up against a barrier of warm steel.

"Come on. My rental car's around the side in the parking lot."

The Hollywood tabloid artists were as relentless as

the European paparazzi. This was D.L.'s fault. It was his way of promoting Ann. Big bucks for her meant more money in his pockets.

Riley grabbed her around the waist and more or less carried her to the car parked in the shade of a palm tree. He drove them back to her condo. When they were safely inside her living room, she turned on him.

"Thanks to you, I've missed an audition for a role I really wanted."

"Don't worry. I know about another role that was made for you and you alone. I promise you're going to love it."

On that cryptic note he strode through the condo to her bedroom and started putting the things she'd already unpacked back in her suitcase. She followed him as far as the doorway.

He was delighting in this!

"I hate to break it to you, Riley, but you have to love your husband to do the housewife thing," she flung sarcastically.

A smile broke out on his unforgettable face. "I think I've been extremely tolerant in forgiving my little injured housewife for running away at the first sign of trouble."

"Stop it, Riley!"

"I've already talked to the manager of the building about your condo. He won't lease it without your approval first. I told him we'd phone to let him know how much of the furnishings you want shipped to Turin."

While she stood there crippled by the sheer force of his presence, he packed up her toiletries from the bathroom. He emerged with her suitcase in hand.

"I'm not going anywhere with you!"

The second she said it, she knew it was a mistake. He started for her and picked her up in a fireman's lift like he'd done before. He was so big and strong and fit, she was held in a viselike grip.

On his way out the door, he reached for her purse on the coffee table. "I think that's everything," he said before pushing it shut with his foot. Then he trekked along the hallway to the elevator.

"Put me down!" she hissed because there were other occupants smiling at them.

He ignored her until they reached the underground car park where he deposited her none too gently in the front seat of the car. Then he shoved everything else in the back seat.

She would have jumped out, but he had a remote that locked the doors. By the time she could find the switch on the panel of the car, he'd already climbed inside and had started the engine.

"This is ridiculous, Riley."

"I agree, but you love doing everything the hard way. It's the story of your life."

"Don't you dare start psychoanalyzing me!"

He flashed her a lancing glance of those silvery eyes. "It's not the most enjoyable experience in the world, but sometimes it's necessary, as I found out through painful personal experience."

"Where are we going? This isn't the way to the airport."

"I have no intention of going there yet. I want you to see something first."

She might be his prisoner, but she refused to feast on his haunting profile. Instead she stared blindly out the side window. Eventually they passed the Santa

Monica city limits sign. He drove further until they reached the lower income district.

He slowed down in front of a tiny bungalow. It resembled dozens of others with postage stamp yards.

"This is where my father lived with his grandparents until they died. He used the money from the sale of the house to buy equipment for his stunts. I never saw the inside of it. According to Bart I lived in trailers and tents with my parents. Somewhere along the way my mother took off. At that point there was just the two of us."

Every word squeezed another tear from her heart.

"I wanted you to see my origins. Now there's someone I want you to meet." He picked up speed. They drove in silence to the parking lot of St. Steven's Hospital.

She knew what it meant. "I—I don't want to meet Sister Francesca."

"She'll want to meet you," he fired back softly. "Don't be afraid. You're not a patient. She won't try any of her psychobabble on the woman I damned on a regular basis."

Cut to the quick she cried, "All I did was turn you down for a dinner date!"

His free hand lifted to the nape of her neck where he massaged her hot skin with gentle insistence. "Nevertheless your rejection traumatized my psyche."

"Don't tell me... No woman had ever told you no before."

"Do I dare answer that truthfully?"

Oh...she'd set herself up for that one.

Without wasting any time he escorted her inside the hospital. The second they approached the nursing station inside she heard one of the nuns cry, "It's Mr. Garrow!"

He smiled. "How are you doing, Sister Angela?"

Her face lit up like a Christmas tree. "I'll tell Sister Francesca you're here. We all saw pictures of you and your wife in the newspaper. She won't believe you came all the way back from Italy to see her!"

She flew around the counter to a private office and knocked on the door.

Pretty soon one young nun after another came out in the hall to see what all the commotion was about. It became clear to Ann the sisters had adored Riley. She heard his name repeated in hushed, excited voices a dozen times at least.

When a middle-aged sister wearing her full white habit suddenly appeared behind the counter, the other nuns dispersed.

Warm brown eyes shone out of a gentle face as she stared at Riley. "I thought we'd gotten rid of you."

Her bold manner with him was a revelation to Ann. She wagered no one else in the world talked to him like that and got away with it.

"I thought you were supposed to be on retreat to recover from me. I guess we both lied. I didn't think a saint did those kinds of things," he teased her.

"You're forgetting your manners, Mr. Garrow."

"So I am." He turned to Ann. Looking at her through shuttered eyes he said, "Sister Francesca, I'd like to introduce you to my wife, Ann."

"How do you do, Mrs. Garrow. I never expected to have the pleasure of meeting such a courageous woman."

Riley chuckled. "I'm sure you didn't."

"I'm very happy to meet you, too," Ann murmured.

The nun's gaze swerved to Riley. "From the newspaper report, you didn't waste any time after you left here."

"As you reminded me more times than I want to remember, 'the clock is ticking, Mr. Garrow. Are you going to let it run out before you've had a chance to really live?' I decided to heed your advice and find out if marriage was all you said it was cracked up to be."

"And is it?"

The salient question hung in the air like a live wire.

Ann held her breath waiting for Riley to tell the nun his bride had run away from him forty-eight hours into their farce of a marriage.

"I think I'll let my wife answer that question. She's the saint in the family and won't tell you lies."

Riley—her heart cried out in exasperation.

He nuzzled her neck. "If Ann's a little shy it's because we're on our honeymoon."

"A shy woman would never have married you, Mr. Garrow."

Riley burst out laughing. Ann tried not to smile but she couldn't help it. In their own ways, they both loved this impossible man. But Sister Francesca wasn't married to him. She would never understand Ann's pain.

Under the circumstances there was only one important thing here. Ann didn't want the older nun to know Riley had resorted to blackmail to accomplish his objective. Let this saint of a woman who'd done so much good trying to help Riley, keep her few illusions.

"We're finding it has its ups and downs, Sister."

Her shrewd eyes rested on Ann. "In your husband's case, if you haven't left him yet that's as good as a sign from heaven."

Another dagger pierced her heart.

Riley reached for Ann's hand and lifted it to the nun's gaze. "The ring's still here," he murmured with a satisfied smile. "When it's no longer there, then I'll be able to answer your question."

Like a mantra, Mitra's warning resounded in her brain. *He'll test your love in many ways. Be prepared.*

"We won't keep you from your duties any longer, Sister. When we leave here, we're going to fly to Prunedale."

Ann's eyes widened in shock.

"She's going to show me the farm where she grew up."

The nun smiled. "I grew up on a farm, too."

"Uh-uh-uh, Sister. You're not supposed to talk about yourself, remember?"

"I made an exception in honor of your wife who has dared to take you on as a lifelong commitment. You will need all the help heaven can give you, my dear. May God bless you both." She made the sign of the cross, then returned to her office.

"She always sounds scarier than she is," Riley whispered as they left the floor. "I wager she's inside that airless cubicle crying tears of happiness."

A saint and a Gypsy had given Ann fair warning. Little did they know they'd been preaching to the converted. Ann knew better than both what kind of a man held her prisoner.

The truth of the matter was, he held all three of them captive in his matchless grasp.

"After we leave Prunedale, we'll fly to San Francisco and leave for home from there."

"Sorry, Riley. I'll be going back to L.A."

"You can't," he said simply.

"That's not for you to decide. We haven't lived in feudal times for centuries."

"Tell that to Prince Enzo. He's waiting for us to return to Turin."

She froze.

"Before you accuse me of using the Prince for my own selfish, nefarious needs, there's something you should know.

"At the behest of Nicco's brother, I had lunch with him the other day while you were at the palace with Callie. It wasn't a social visit.

"He's dealing with a socioeconomic issue that has become political and controversial in nature. Recently he has called in various experts to form a steering committee to look into the problem and make suggestions to form policy. To my surprise he's asked me to be a part of that task force."

Was no one immune to her husband's impact? Not even a royal prince? Maybe Ann was having some kind of strange dream.

"He wants you a part of the project, too."

She rubbed her eyes in defeat.

"When Nicco brought me back to the barge, I was eager to tell you about it and see what you thought, but I'm afraid personal matters escalated out of control. Considering how much you esteem him and Nicco, I felt this had to take priority over our personal problems.

"He's expecting an answer one way or the other.

Since it wasn't something I cared to discuss over the phone with you long distance, I came after you.''

Riley had flown all the way to L.A. because of Enzo? It was like suffering a second death.

''Here's Anna's bottle. She's so happy you're back home to feed her!'' While Ann cradled the baby in her arms, Callie sat across the couch from her eyeing her anxiously. Now that dinner was over, the dogs were nowhere to be found.

''I saw Riley and Enzo riding past the lodge on horseback a few minutes ago. Before they return, tell me what's going on!''

''I only came back with Riley out of courtesy to Enzo. Once I've met with him later, I'm planning to fly home to California in the morning. If I stay in L.A., there are a lot of opportunities to teach English and drama at a private school. Should a decent script come along, I still might consider it.''

''Ann—I want to know why you're leaving Riley.''

''You mean Nicco hasn't told you yet?''

''If my husband knows something, he hasn't breathed a word.''

Of course he hasn't. His disappointment in Riley runs too deep.

''I don't want to talk about it either, Callie.''

''He must have hurt you terribly,'' her sister whispered.

She kissed Anna's cheek. ''I'll get over it. I'm just sorry you and Nicco had to be involved in a situation that should never have happened. It's put so many people out, and it's all my fault.''

''Stop talking like that. We're family.''

''True, but I'm the one who always has the crises,

or creates them. Look what happened when I forced you to come to Italy in my place.''

''I found my life! That's what happened and you know it! I'll be thankful to you forever.''

''I'm glad it had a happy ending for you, Callie.''

''Riley said you flew to Prunedale before you came home.''

''That was his idea.''

''How was it?''

''Painful. The Montagues are harvesting the apples on the farm right now. Riley didn't help things by asking Mrs. Montague if he could pick some. It brought back a lot of memories,'' her voice trembled. ''He ate all the garden delicious and left the winter bananas for me.''

''You always did love those best. Did you see Dr. Wood?''

''Yes. He was spaying the Landau's new golden retriever.''

''So old Topper finally died.''

''Doesn't everything?''

Hot tears gushed from her eyes. She got up from the couch. ''Do you mind taking care of Anna? I need to go upstairs before Enzo comes in and finds me like this.''

Callie's eyes filled with tears. She jumped to her feet and threw her arms around her. ''I wish I could help.''

''So do I.''

Ann handed the baby to her sister, then left for the east wing on a run.

An hour later Riley came in the bedroom for a quick shower. He announced they would be meeting with Enzo in Callie's office as soon as he was ready.

Thankfully Ann had already showered and dressed in a tailored black suit with a black and white print blouse. Her makeup disguised the worst of the circles under her eyes. For once she wore her hair in a French twist secured with a tortoise shell comb. She wanted to look her best for Nicco's brother.

Callie called it Ann's untouchable, immaculate look.

She supposed it was because she'd never fixed her hair this way in front of Riley that he studied her with such intense scrutiny before disappearing into the bathroom.

They hadn't spoken to each other since deboarding the plane in Turin. She'd told him on the jet she would be going back to California the next day. It appeared the message had finally sunk in.

Not wanting to spend another second in his presence that wasn't absolutely necessary, Ann left the bedroom and went back downstairs to Callie's office to wait.

"There you are." Dark blond Enzo got up from Callie's desk to hug her. He was still dressed in his riding clothes. His brown eyes swept over her in male admiration.

It reminded her of the night a year ago when he'd picked her as his bride for the *Who Wants to Marry a Prince?* benefit. When he smiled, his dimples appeared. He truly was Prince Charming with no hidden dark side.

"You look like a princess tonight."

"Thank you. Is Maria with you?"

"No. She knew I was coming here on business, so she took Alberto to visit her parents. Sit down, Ann."

She found an upholstered chair opposite the desk.

"I appreciate your willingness to meet with me

when I know you and Riley are still on your honeymoon. He told me about your accident. To look this lovely, you must be feeling better."

"I'm fine now, thank you. The bruises are fading. The good news is I didn't ruin the bike."

"I'm afraid that was your husband's last concern. When I talked to him, I could tell he was shaken."

"I've found out Riley's the patriarchal type who prefers to do all the driving." It was a source of more friction while they were in Prunedale.

"Only until you're fully healed," Riley interjected. Apparently he'd heard them talking on his way inside the room.

Enzo rose to his feet and shook Riley's hand before indicating he should sit next to Ann. She refused to acknowledge her husband. Fresh from the shower, he smelled wonderful. She knew he would be looking drop dead gorgeous in the black silk shirt and gray trousers she'd seen hanging in the closet earlier.

"I'll get right to the point so I don't keep you too long." His gaze leveled on Ann.

"Nicco and Callie told me about Boiko, who came to the preserve with the squirrel."

His topic of conversation surprised her as much as the gravity of his tone.

"Later, I heard that you and Riley drove him home with a rabbit and discovered him living in an encampment on the outskirts."

She nodded.

"I know. I've been there several times before and was there again yesterday with some parliament officials walking around. The plight of the Romanies across Europe is nothing new. Like you, I'm outraged to see them treated like alien beings. But when it's happening in my own monarchy, something has to be done.''

''I agree, Enzo!'' she cried fervently, clasping her hands together.

''It's not going to happen overnight, and whatever measures are taken, they won't ever be enough. But it *will* be a beginning.''

Forgetting the promise to herself to ignore Riley, her head turned in his direction. Their eyes met. His expression was as solemn as Enzo's. She looked back at the Prince once more.

''On the barge I had the opportunity to talk with Mitra and her relatives in Italian. It was very enlightening and encouraging to learn that her family has been absorbed into our culture enough that they have jobs and live in decent housing. Up until now, only those who've come into some money have been able to enjoy some of the benefits that a normal citizen of our country takes for granted.''

He frowned. ''The vast majority that don't have money will always be on the fringe of society. Without being able to speak the language, they can't go to school or get jobs. It's a vicious circle that goes round without end.

''Riley has had the unique experience of being a close observer in a Gypsy household for seventeen years of his life. There are many dialects of course, many refugees from many nations, but he speaks their language and understands their customs.

''Just as important, he attended school here in Italy for ten years and is intimately familiar with our education system from a foreigner's point of view. He's also fluent in English, Italian, Portuguese and Russian.''

Riley's language skills didn't surprise Ann, not with his keen gifts and intelligence.

"For someone like myself who is looking for the right people to put a plan into action to help these people, your husband is a godsend." He sat forward.

"I've asked him if he'll head up the committee I've chosen to make suggestions and come up with an initial plan for the first stage. It would be a lifetime career appointment. Once you start to deal with the Gypsies, you must see it through over a generation in order to establish trust.

"The money will come from an ongoing foundation my father started years ago to aid our people. More money will be funneled in for the project when a budget has been calculated.

"Until such time as this new Italian-Gypsy Alliance grows to the point a larger facility is needed, the east wing of this palace will serve as the headquarters."

His eyes searched hers for a long moment. "Riley has told me he'll accept the position as President of the Alliance on one condition…"

CHAPTER TEN

SUDDENLY she knew what was coming.

Her heart pounded so hard and fast she thought she was going to pass out.

Next to you, Mitra is the most important woman in my life.

Ann knew Riley's heart went out to the Gypsies. Enzo couldn't possibly understand what he'd done by offering Riley this position.

Her husband would see it as a way to pay back Mitra for her years of selfless love. He would view it as an unprecedented opportunity to help the thousands of poverty-stricken Boiko's who had no tools to bridge the terrible gap society intentionally kept wide-open. Riley's career as a racing pro would mean nothing in comparison to this.

The only problem was, Riley knew that she knew it, and he was counting on that knowledge to prevent her from divorcing him.

Another form of blackmail.

Two powerful men were staring at her, awaiting her reaction.

She wondered how Nicco felt about it. Was he wounded over Riley's defection? Did he know Enzo had offered Riley the presidency of the alliance yet? Would it create tension between the two brothers who had always seemed so close?

"Your silence lets me know you're feeling over-whelmed," Enzo murmured. "I wouldn't blame you if you disliked me for ruining your honeymoon with such a weighty matter.''

He stood up. "I'm going to go home so you and Riley can discuss the condition he has laid down. Call me tomorrow or the next day when you've come to a decision. I'll let myself out. Good night."

He kissed her cheek, then disappeared through the doors. Ann turned to Riley, ready to do battle.

"Don't you dare put this on me or try to make me take on any guilt for what you do or don't do as the result of my divorcing you."

He gave one of those elegant shrugs of his shoulders. "If you want one that badly, I won't stand in your way. That wasn't the condition, by the way."

His shocking comment delivered in such an offhand manner staggered her.

"The old Gypsies can't be changed. It's their children who need help towards emancipation. The east wing of the palace has enough rooms to run the foundation with all its facets and still have space for a classroom.

"The first stage of a project like this must include a working model for the community to examine. Boiko and others like him would be the perfect candidates.

"I must have a teacher who before any other qualification is free of bias. The Gypsies aren't the world's greatest paranoiacs without a reason. You made a breakthrough with Boiko without speaking a word of Romany. Dr. Donatti told me he's come to the preserve several times looking for you.

"That rare connection could be the beginning of something exciting. Your degree in English, plus your acting talent makes you the perfect choice. You could learn Romany as you go along. With my help in the translation department, there's no telling where this could lead. The preserve is a natural playground for the children. They'd be comfortable here.

"The goal is to prepare them to attend regular school. It would mean a huge commitment on your part."

His black brows furrowed. "The wrong teacher could ruin everything. It's a setback I wouldn't relish, and it would rebound on Enzo whose vision is commendable in the highest sense.

"That's why my acceptance was conditional on your signing a five year teaching contract. It would take you five years with someone like Boiko before he'd be ready to trust another teacher."

He got to his feet. "Before you accuse me of blackmail, remember this is Enzo's brainchild, not mine. You heard what he said. He's already gathered a committee. Someone else will accept the position and do the job if I don't.

"Much as I would like to accept, I can't go into this alone, and you're the only person I trust.

"What an irony that the one woman I need not only doesn't trust me, she can't wait to be free of me.

"Callie's going to let me take her car to the marina tonight. I'll be back at six in the morning with the things you've left on the barge. I'm sure you'll want to pack them for your flight home."

Ann had gone numb. Now Nicco's brother was going to have a terrible impression of her, too. "Did you tell Enzo what your condition was?"

"No, and he didn't ask. One thing I've learned about the Tescotti brothers. They're very private people who give others the same courtesy. I've never met finer men. It's been a privilege to know them.''

His eyes wandered over her as if memorizing her. ''Your face has lost color. You must be getting a migraine. Go to bed, Ann.''

It's been a privilege to know them.
It's been a privilege to know them.

Ann came awake with the blood pounding in her ears, gasping for breath. There was this oppressive heaviness in the region of her chest. She shot out of bed wondering if she was having a heart attack. Her body had broken out in a cold sweat.

The headache that had forced her to take pain killer was supposed to have kept her asleep all night. One glance at her watch indicated it was only ten after two in the morning.

She clung to the bedpost with both hands willing her body to calm down, but it refused.

Once Riley dropped her things off, she'd never seen him again.

That was the reason for the pain.

To never look in his eyes again—to never be in his presence again—was unthinkable.

Suddenly the concerns of the past didn't matter anymore. Like Sister Francesca and Mitra, she loved him pure and simply. He'd put those two women through hell, yet they'd continued to love him and be there for him without strings.

She would have to do the same and never count the cost because a life without him in it, was no life at all.

Without wasting another second, she rang for a taxi, then alerted the security guard at the private gate to let it come on through to the east entrance of the palace.

The light from a full moon reflecting off the river made it unnecessary for Riley to turn on the lamp. He sat hunched on the couch with his hands clasped between his knees. The unopened bottle of whiskey stared back at him from the coffee table.

Mitra had given it to him for a going away present the night before he'd had to leave for Russia with his father.

I want you to keep this with you wherever you go. Every time you are tempted to open it, remember that it represents your father's sickness.

By some miracle, or evil design, however he chose to look at it, the bottle had survived twelve years in tact.

The first time he'd intended to drain the contents was when Sister Francesca had caught him with it in his hands and had confiscated it for safe keeping. Being the honest soul she was, he'd found it wrapped in his suitcase when he'd prepared to leave the hospital.

Tonight was the second time he was ready to break it open, if only to blot Ann from his consciousness for a few hours.

Suddenly a noise distracted his morose thoughts. He had the distinct impression someone was outside the cabin prowling around. Instinct drove him to all fours. He made it to the wall next to the door and flattened himself against it.

Footsteps came closer. There was a knock. "Riley?" a familiar voice called out. "It's Ann! Can you hear me? Open up!"

He undid the lock and flung the door wide, causing

her to cry out. Her hand went to her throat. "You scared me!"

Though he knew he'd frightened her, her green eyes looked at him with a hunger he'd never seen in them before. His heart skittered all over the place.

She stood there with the moonlight bathing her flowing blond hair. It illuminated the breathtaking mold of her curves and long legs. The first time he'd laid eyes on her, the beauty of her classic features had filled his vision so he was blind to any other woman after that.

But so much had happened since then, it was her inner beauty he was seeing now. She glowed.

His body grew weak. "What in the hell are you doing here in the middle of the night without letting me know you were coming? I could have hurt you," his voice shook.

"It was a risk I was willing to take to be with the husband I love more than life itself." Her hands lifted to his chest. "But I have to say you really do swear too much, Riley. Honestly, darling, is that any way to greet your wife? The woman who's joined at the hip with you forever?"

He felt her soft arms glide around his neck with a sense of wonder.

"I've been a fool." She kissed his hair, his eyes, his jaw, his mouth. "For better, for worse, I love you, Riley Garrow. I love you. It doesn't matter if you can't say the words back. I'll take everything you *can* say. Everything you're willing to give me.

"No more talk now, my love. I want to show you just how much you mean to me. Come to bed."

She grasped his hand and took the lead. Riley didn't

remember his feet touching the ground because his soul was soaring.

Riley's loving had made her feel immortal. After satisfying each other's needs for hours, he'd finally fallen asleep. Ann couldn't sleep. She didn't want to.

Besides being the most wonderful man in existence, he was the most beautiful. Just looking at him brought her intense pleasure. Though he was in a deep sleep, his arms never let her go.

The knowledge that she would be able to luxuriate like this against him for the rest of their lives filled her with inexpressible joy.

As she studied his masculine features, the black curly hair she loved to touch, she grew impatient to know his possession again. Unable to wait for him to wake up, she began kissing him.

His powerful legs moved first, tangling with the silken length of hers. His hands began rediscovering her body. Then he was giving her kiss for kiss until the earth shook and they became one pulsating entity.

Much later, "Where do you think you're going?" His possessive arms wouldn't allow her to ease away from him.

"To fix you something to eat. Do you realize it's after one o'clock?"

"We'll do it together," he whispered. "But before you leave this bed, there's something I have to tell you."

She put a finger to his lips. "I already know. You've told me in a hundred different ways since you showed up for dinner with Nicco. I'm not the linguist you are, but I've finally figured out your language."

His eyes had turned a liquid silver. "The word love

never meant anything to me, Ann, but it does now. People who speak English use it to describe anything and everything, robbing it of its full weight.

"Do you know there isn't a word for love in Romany? Mitra told me its real meaning is too important to be used indiscriminately. You have to find other ways to express it."

Ann cradled his cheek with her hand. "I think you've found every one of them because I've never known love like this before. Mitra warned me you would test my love. Now I understand.

"She didn't mean you didn't love me, but she knew I would have to learn to interpret the way you expressed it, or all was lost. In her own way, Sister Francesca was telling me the same thing. What remarkable women have loved you!"

"You most of all," he murmured emotionally.

"When you say such nice things to me, there isn't anything I wouldn't do for you. Now I'm going to stop being lazy and make us lunch."

"I'll help."

They drew on their robes and left the bedroom.

"What's this?" She took a detour to the coffee table and lifted the bottle of whiskey.

Riley grinned. "There's a story attached. I'll tell you about it later. All that matters right now is that the man you're looking at is madly in love with his wife. I don't need to carry it around with me anymore."

He took it from her and headed for the kitchen. She watched in surprise as he undid the lid and poured the contents down the sink. After tossing the empty bottle in the wastebasket, he turned to her and held out his arms.

She went running.

*   *   *

When they came to a stop, Ann got off her bike and removed her helmet. From the high mountain pasture, she could see Locarno on Lake Maggiore over in the next lush green valley. They were almost to the border of Switzerland where adorable chalets and soft air carrying the sounds of alpenhorns made her feel as if she'd stepped inside the pages of a fairy tale.

This was the first bike trip for the four of them. Callie didn't want Ann to be worn out, so they'd planned to sleep in Locarno, then make a loop back to Turin the next day.

A pair of rock-hard masculine arms slid around her waist from behind. Even through their leathers, she felt his strong heartbeat against her back.

"What do you think?" He kissed her neck.

"I can't describe it. It's too beautiful. This is too exciting. I'm too happy. Oh, Riley—" she whirled around and grabbed him. "I feel so euphoric, I might just float away."

"There's no way I'm going to let that happen."

Their mouths came together in passion. This was the kind of rapture they'd been sharing since she'd gone after her husband in the middle of the night a month ago.

Now that Riley had accepted the appointment Enzo had offered, their lives had been transformed. They'd moved in the east wing of the palace, but still spent their weekends on the barge.

Every minute they weren't busy talking and planning for the Alliance, they were in each other's arms.

"Anytime you two want to leave, just let us know," Nicco teased before devouring Callie.

"How about it, Mrs. Garrow? Are you ready for a night in front of a cozy fire?"

"Oh, yes!" She kissed him passionately. "Callie's crazy about this place where we're going to stay."

"Then let's get going. There's something important I want to talk to you about."

He sounded mysterious. She sensed it didn't have to do with business.

They took off ahead of Callie and Nicco. Halfway down the mountain Nicco shot ahead of them. He rode like the wind. Ann could tell Riley wanted to join him.

She started to slow down and made a signal that he should go on without her. Through his face guard she saw him flash her an ecstatic smile before he took off like a rocket.

It was sheer poetry watching the two of them do the fanciest riding she'd ever seen in her life. They were like two boys who'd exploded out the school doors to begin their summer vacation. Freedom.

At this point Callie had caught up to her and they'd both stopped to watch. "You can almost hear them whooping it up, can't you?" her sister said in a laughing voice.

"You sure can," Ann replied. "I say if you can't beat 'em, join 'em. Let's go!"

"You're on!"

They revved their engines and took off down the rest of the mountain road. Now it was the guys' turn to watch them. Callie popped an amazing wheelie that went on forever. By the time their exhilarating ride came to an end at the bottom, their husbands were clapping for her expertise.

One day Ann intended to reap that reward, but it

would take many more hours on her bike to be that accomplished.

Later that night, satiated by a delicious meal, she and Riley lay on the floor in front of the fire. For a while they didn't talk, only gazed into each other's eyes and touched each other.

She would never tire of looking at her husband.

"You and I have discussed everything except our own children," Riley began.

"It's what I want more than anything in the world!" she cried softly. "How many were you thinking of?"

"One to start with, sweetheart."

"I can't promise that."

At first he frowned, then he threw back his head and laughed. The next thing she knew he'd pulled her on top of him.

His eyes danced. "Twins. Wouldn't that be something."

"Does the possibility scare you?"

He sobered. "Not if you're their mother."

"Darling—"

He'd given her his heart for safe keeping. He'd done it on faith. It was up to her if he ever truly learned to trust in that powerful, magnificent, sacred, wonderful, yet most fragile emotion called love.

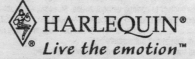

If you enjoyed what you just read,
then we've got an offer you can't resist!

Take 2 bestselling love stories FREE!

Plus get a FREE surprise gift!

Clip this page and mail it to Harlequin Reader Service®

IN U.S.A.	IN CANADA
3010 Walden Ave.	P.O. Box 609
P.O. Box 1867	Fort Erie, Ontario
Buffalo, N.Y. 14240-1867	L2A 5X3

YES! Please send me 2 free Harlequin Romance® novels and my free surprise gift. After receiving them, if I don't wish to receive anymore, I can return the shipping statement marked cancel. If I don't cancel, I will receive 6 brand-new novels every month, before they're available in stores! In the U.S.A., bill me at the bargain price of $3.34 plus 25¢ shipping & handling per book and applicable sales tax, if any*. In Canada, bill me at the bargain price of $3.80 plus 25¢ shipping & handling per book and applicable taxes**. That's the complete price and a savings of 10% off the cover prices—what a great deal! I understand that accepting the 2 free books and gift places me under no obligation ever to buy any books. I can always return a shipment and cancel at any time. Even if I never buy another book from Harlequin, the 2 free books and gift are mine to keep forever.

186 HDN DNTX
386 HDN DNTY

Name	(PLEASE PRINT)	
Address	Apt.#	
City	State/Prov.	Zip/Postal Code

* Terms and prices subject to change without notice. Sales tax applicable in N.Y.
** Canadian residents will be charged applicable provincial taxes and GST.
   All orders subject to approval. Offer limited to one per household and not valid to
   current Harlequin Romance® subscribers.
® are registered trademarks of Harlequin Enterprises Limited.

HROM02 ©2001 Harlequin Enterprises Limited

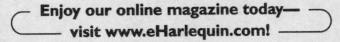

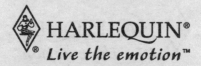

WHAT WOMEN WANT!

Dare to Dream...

Every woman has dreams—long-cherished hopes, deep desires, or perhaps just little everyday wishes!

In this brand-new miniseries from

Harlequin Romance®

we're delighted to present a series of fresh, lively and compelling stories by some of our most popular authors—all exploring the truth about what women *really* want.

May: THE BRIDESMAID'S REWARD by Liz Fielding (#3749)

June: SURRENDER TO A PLAYBOY by Renee Roszel (#3752)

July: WITH THIS BABY... by Caroline Anderson (#3756)

August: THE BILLIONAIRE BID by Leigh Michaels (#3759)

Look out for many more emotionally exhilarating stories by your favorite Harlequin Romance® *authors, coming soon!*

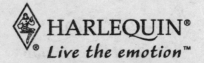

HARLEQUIN®

Live the emotion™

Visit us at www.eHarlequin.com

HRWWWA3